To
Brian A Craig
with my best wishes

Michael Kulikowski
London, 22 May 2007

**EMPEROR OF
THE GALATIANS**

To my wife Nina

Special thanks to my special friends
– Samo and Mirjana

EMPEROR OF THE GALATIANS

a novel by Mihajlo Kažić

Translated by Sheila Sofrenović
Illustrations by the author

Florida Academic Press
Gainesville and London

Copyright © 2005 by Florida Academic Press

All rights reserved. No part of this book may be reproduced or transmitted in any form or manner, by any means, mechanical, electronic or other including by photocopying, recording or via information storage and retrieval systems, without the express permission of Florida Academic Press, except for the inclusion of brief quotations in reviews.

Published in the United States of America by Florida Academic Press, Gainesville, FL, September 2005
Cover prepared by Gordon Woolf
Cover: Soldiers, detail of the frescoes "Betrayal of Judas" beginning of the 13th century, Patriarchate of Peć, Serbia. Photo by Branislav Strugar used with his permission. Permit for use as the cover photo by Serbian Orthodox Church, No. 116/2005 of February 18, 2005.
Originally written in Serbian, this book was first published in 1993 by Kiepenheuer (Leipzig, Germany), as *Der Kaiser der Galater*.

Library of Congress Cataloging-in-Publication Data

Kazic, Mihajlo, 1960-
    Emperor of the Galatians : a novel / by Mihajlo Kazic ; translated by Sheila Sofrenovic ; illustrations by the author.
       p. cm.
    Originally written in Serbian, this book was first published in 1993 by Kiepenheuer (Leipzig, Germany), as Der Kaiser der Galater.
    ISBN 1-890357-15-4
    1. Galatians--Fiction. I. Sofrenovic, Sheila. II. Title.

PG1419.21.A96E47 2005
891.3'236--dc22

2005012668

Contents

Prologue	*1*
The First Day	*3*
Opening The First Six Seals	*5*
Enemies of The Earthly Kingdom	*11*
I Can Touch You With My Hand	*17*
The First Woman	*21*
Unsigned Letters	*25*
The Infected Shirt	*31*
New Future	*33*
The Leaves Of The Wind	*37*
A Dog's Death	*41*
Preparation For Death	*45*
Mathematics Is Music	*47*
Life Is A Dream	*51*
False Bottom	*55*
The Morning Hours Have Golden Mouths	*59*
Secret Message	*63*
Journey To Rome	*65*
White Powder	*67*
Kristina, My Beloved	*71*
Confession	*75*
A Gnashing Of Teeth	*77*
Mark On The Forehead	*81*
A Nervous Horse	*85*
A Clock That Doesn't Tell The Time	*87*

When The Sun Was God	*89*
The Best Place In Rome	*95*
A Mistake Corrected	*97*
The Night Wind	*99*
The Old Oak	*105*
Letters Visible And Letters Invisible	*107*
Everything Will Come To An End Anyway	*111*
A Happy Childhood	*115*
Color Number Seventeen	*117*
Accidental Death	*119*
Double Death	*123*
The Secret Of Dead And Living Words	*127*
Fire Spots	*131*
An Unknown Scent	*139*
Tale Of A Beautiful Witch	*141*
A Place Where The Dead Talk	*145*
The Puddle Which Made Dogs Growl	*151*
Time Of Cold Rains	*155*
A Man With No Friends	*159*
Poison	*161*
We'll Both Survive	*165*
A Starry Sky	*167*
King Of Fire And King Of Shadows	*171*
The Book Of Wisdom	*173*
The Boy Who Wanted To Be Cuddled	*175*
Rushing River	*179*
Walled-up Windows	*181*
Division Of Power	*187*
The Distant Unknown	*191*
Tale Of The Emperor's Recovery	*193*
Hiding From The Voices	*201*
Battle In Heaven	*205*
Song Of Songs	*209*

1
Prologue

THIS IS A DREAM about the all-powerful ruler Bonifacio, two imperial ministers and three poor young men. It was dreamed in Hebrew, but written down in Galatian. Many will wonder why it was not written down the way it was dreamed when it is known that the Jews revere their books so much that they dare not touch their oldest writings by hand, but use a silver wand, moving its tip from letter to letter. Sadly, there are nations who burn their books. And as if this were not enough, during these rampages they regularly burn all the books in Hebrew they get their hands on.

The Galatians are a warlike people. They have a very high opinion of themselves though others mock them. It is said of them that they reek of onion and brandy, that they are wild men and barely literate. Eternally poor, the Galatians consider it a sin to throw away bread or burn a book. Whenever attacked by an enemy, they abandon what little they own and flee. The only load they hoist onto their scraggy horses are their books written in a strange alphabet. In times of war, starving, they retreat before the enemy, with their books. So it is easier to set fire to the Galatians' houses than their books.

Fire destroys everything. But then everything came into being in times beyond recall when red flames poured through the white fire and inscribed what you read now in red letters on a white background. And every copy of this book is protected by a good angel who prevents it falling into the hands of an evil-wisher. In case of need, all the fiery letters can jumble up and deceive the would-be reader.

This poor unfortunate could spend hours poring over them, and see nothing. In the end, his eyes would close from fatigue, and he would fall asleep over the open book.

This is a dream about the all-powerful ruler Bonifacio, who was outlived by this story about him. He held sway over the great city of Rome, and thence the entire kingdom of the earth. It is in that distant age of prosperity that this tale of men and demons starts.

Dreamed in the town of Nuestra Señora la Reina de Los Angeles in the summer, 1987 years after the birth of Jesus Christ or the year 7497 when the world began.

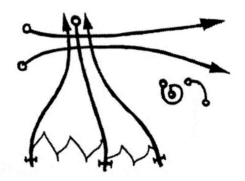

2
The First Day

**meaning Sunday for the Jews,
and Monday for the Galatians**

THE SOUND OF RAPID FOOTSTEPS ECHOED down the long corridors in the State Administration Centre. At the end of the working day only Mr José Alkorta, Minister of Education, was left sitting in his office. This was an unusual room on the ground floor of a protruding wing of the building, which cut into a small wood. Almost separated from the rest of the huge edifice, its jutting position seemed to make it a part both of the wood and the building. The French windows in the room led straight out into a spacious garden. As a rule, this tall, thin, slightly stooping man spent all his time in a world consisting of carefully nurtured plants in the garden and an office with furniture made out of cherry wood. On his desk, as a mark of extreme respect, there was a silk imperial flag. Around the flag's silver stand an unusual ribbon bearing a six-pointed yellow star was knotted. Inside the star was a red embroidered rose with six petals.

What the honorable Mr Alkorta did so late every day, no one could say for certain. The guards said that nobody was waiting for him at home anyway, and that he would hang around till deep into the night and wander round the garden.

"He's forever writing something. A real weirdo. When out for a stroll, he looks down at the ground, in the direction in which he's walking. You just wait for him to trip over his feet. At least he could look up at the sky, then you'd be sure what sort of man he is."

"He's a strange fish, that one," the gardener said admiringly. "He planted the flowers himself this spring. He waters them regularly. He often gets carried away and even talks to them."

True to form, Mr Alkorta, today, too, at the end of official working hours, collected all the papers from his desk and took out some other documents from the cupboard. He bent his head and started to write on the empty sheets of paper. The phone rang.

"Hello? Alkorta here."
"Mr Alkorta, it's me."
"What is it, Federico?"
"Mr Alkorta, I just wanted to ask you, is it OK for tonight?"
"You mean, to leave earlier?"
"Yes!"
"We've already agreed everything. I'll come back by taxi. It's no problem."
"Oh, thank you, sir. You've done me a great favor. You know, we drivers like to…"
"That's all right, Federico" — José interrupted him. "You just have a good time. See you tomorrow."

José carried on writing, but now more slowly and with increasingly frequent interruptions. His thin, bony face took on an absent look. As time passed, this absent-mindedness passed. It was already nightfall when he put down the pen, resolved to set off home. He checked whether there was a driver available.

Apart from the duty telephone operator and the night guard, there was no one in the building. José ordered a taxi and threw his raincoat round his shoulders. He said goodbye to the two men as he passed and went out into the street.

"Honestly, it takes all sorts!" José couldn't hear the conversation at the reception desk. "I wouldn't stay a minute longer than I have to."
"Yes, but we don't get anything for overtime!"
"You think he does?"
"Listen, mate, he's different from the likes of us two! We could lose our jobs over nothing. But who keeps an eye on him? He doesn't have that sort of problem on his mind."

It was a rather cold night. José stood in front of the building whose façade was lit up by a granite cross and an eagle, symbols of the Holy Roman Empire.

3
Opening The First Six Seals

WHEN THE TAXI STOPPED, José quickly got into the back. The very appearance of the shabby cab made him feel depressed. Mumbling his address, he settled back into the torn seat. He suddenly gave a start at the thought that the general dirt might stain his suit. The much-used, dented vehicle set off with a deafening roar. The imperial minister sat helpless, firmly convinced that the best thing was to move as little as possible.

"Just my bad luck to get this foreigner" — his thoughts rambled. "Moroccan, or whatever he is. Who on earth gave him a work permit? I bet he hardly knows the language either. Just as long as we get home without a smash-up. Goodness, how many people come to Rome to seek their fortune. Illiterate, don't know the language, no papers, no citizenship. The poorest of the poor. The only thing they do have is a load of children."

Autumn was beginning to set in. The night was cold and the sky clear and quite cloudless. The perfect, full moon radiated a cold and unfathomable light. The brilliance of the clear night and the limitless heavens scattered with stars carried José away. His gaze fixed on the heights above, he forgot the Moroccan, the past day and his duties.

"Excuse me, sir" — the stranger's voice roused him from his reverie. "Are you by any chance from Galatia?"

He squinted into the mirror, awaiting a reply.

José was confused! He nodded and continued to say nothing.

Is it possible? That a man like this should find out?

In all the twenty years he had been in Rome, nobody had even guessed. True, José was only a young man when he arrived from distant Galatia. From Suvi Potok, a hamlet off the beaten track in an area at the end of the world. It was there, as a child, that he had led the cattle out to pasture in meadows that were right on the border. Everything in that region had always been wild and untamed. Wizened orchards, vineyards with sour grapes, and furrowed roads that turned to mud in autumn. The grass was tough and sharp, you couldn't walk across the meadows barefoot. In that land nothing prospered but plums. On the front of their log shacks the peasants carved strange signs to ward off dark forces. This drew your eyes and diverted attention from the house to the sign. Spells cannot penetrate these bewitching eyes of men and demons because the eyes deceive and the house thus stays protected. For Galatia is a land of evil spirits. There they still give double names to their children. One is the real name, bestowed out of love, and the other defective and ugly. From birth itself, people always address each other by the uglier names to ward off misfortune. The evil spirits then attack the false names and the children grow up safe and sound, with their own beautiful names which, to this day, they do not utter, but which are entered into the state registers.

It was a fact that the minister's real name was Belisario Karamark. While he was still a child, they called him Vesko, to ensure that Belisario survived, and Vesko did not. They chose his real name after some ancient military leader of the Eastern Empire, which turned out to be a good sign. Vesko was not yet very old when a serious epidemic swept his native Galatia. He lost both brothers and both parents. Then he was given the family name of Karamark, after the man who took him in as a disease-stricken child. For days, they all thought that Vesko, too, would die. But by some miracle, he pulled through, after two years spent in a sickbed.

The old women said that the imperial general, whose name he bore, had protected Vesko from death. Lost in admiration, they swore that little Vesko would live to be the equal of that ancient hero. When he arrived in Rome, as a hungry and frail young man, he changed his first and last names. He became José Alkorta. He wanted to protect himself both from the forces of evil and gloomy memories. But now an unknown driver had uncovered his lifelong secret.

José angrily glanced towards the inside mirror to get a better look at the driver. The old car was shaking. The short weasel's tail which the Moroccan had tied to the mirror swung to and fro at the frequent jerking of the car. The minister turned his eyes to the tail. He pulled himself together. He looked at the mirror again. The tail was swinging irritatingly. José felt uncomfortable. The driver continued to stare at him inquisitively in the mirror. Beneath the black moustache you could make out a broad grin and a gold tooth.

"How did you guess that?" he asked the driver. "Was it my accent?"
"No. I recognize people by their appearance."
José fell silent.
"Good grief, is it possible that my appearance gives me away?"
Unconsciously, he put his hand to his big nose and wide cheekbones.
"By my appearance, you say?" the minister repeated.
"Yes! That's what the man looked like in the room next to mine. He died, poor soul. A very unnatural death."
"An unnatural death?" said José in surprise. "Alas, every death is natural."
"Not this one." the Moroccan continued in a deep voice. "He suffered all week long. I was going to work one morning, and there he was lying in the street. They asked how he got to the street. He didn't know. He simply said some hand had squeezed him till he choked. It dragged him off somewhere where he spoke to his dad. The next day someone again shouted from his room, he struggled. He was all in a cold sweat. Run, save the man. He went all stiff. He sprouted a beard in front of my eyes. He couldn't bend his hands at the wrist, or his legs at the knee. He was alive, but dead at the same time. A bit later, he was better. When, next day, he started howling. Some man from his fainting state wanted to carry him off. He flailed his arms in the air, fought back. Seven days he took to die. In the end he rolled up his eyes. He died for good. Went mad, they said. I felt sorry for him. Poor guy, all he did was write things. Left all his papers."
"Papers?" José gave a start.
"But they were all in your language. No one can read."
"Could I see them?" José interrupted.
This seemed to be exactly what the Moroccan had been waiting for. He suddenly accelerated towards the suburbs.
They had long since left the wide streets behind them. Finally, they came to a poorly lit, dilapidated building. Beside the half-demolished front door a rusty board hung which said Yellow Roses Street - no.32. The Moroccan gave a sign with his eyes. Without speaking, they entered the cold, spit-spattered hall. The stench of rancid fat was mixed with the

smell of damp walls. It was all José could do to prevent himself from throwing up. In the distance the sound of a kettledrum echoed. A child could be heard crying. A shudder ran through José. They climbed the dark stairs without a word. On the second floor the driver kicked open an unlocked door. Switching on the light, they went into a small, airless room. Water was dripping from the ceiling. Stinking water spread all over the floor. The walls were not whitewashed and they emanated the sickly sweet smell of death. José could not breathe this tainted air. He hurried to the window and threw it open with a sudden jerk. He took a deep breath with relief.

He stayed there for some time leaning out of the window. The crying of the child and the shouts of its parents in a strange language reached him from some apartment on the ground floor.

"Rooms remember their dead," he reflected, looking at the dark roofs of the neighboring buildings. The tin cocks on the weather vanes shone eerily in the moonlight.

When he turned, he saw the worried face of the Moroccan, who handed him a pile of bound papers. After untying the knot, José leafed through some of the sheets. He took them over to the dull light. He did not understand what was written there. With rapid movements he turned over the papers written in black ink. His eyes came to rest on one sheet that looked like an ordinary letter. This was the only legible manuscript written in Galatian.

Dear brother Demetrakos,

This year of grace our emperor Bonifacio will fall ill. Although old and evil, he will survive. Such is the will of Lilith. The mission is not yet complete. Three young men from three corners of the earth have set out for Rome to cure the emperor. Not one knows his assignment. They will carry it out successfully, while their enemies will fall. We must help these three youths.

With love and ΦΚΤ
Emperor of the Galatians

Sensing that someone was watching him, José raised his head. In the doorway he saw a fat, slovenly woman with an ugly scab on her nose. She stood with her hands on her hips.

"Is there an address?" the Moroccan interrupted him.

"Yes. I'll work this out," replied José, nodding to him that they should go.

Then the woman broke in:

"I, sir," she said in a nasty voice, "am the chief janitor and I still haven't received my wages."

"Everything has been paid," the Moroccan interrupted. At that moment, her forced politeness vanished. Her face contorted with anger. She slapped her backside with all her strength:

"That's how much has been paid! Beggar, swindler! He didn't have a bean! Nobody gives a damn that I have to respect the regulations. It's me the area supervisor will come chasing after, not you, you good-for-nothing foreigners!"

José held out several bank notes to her. The woman immediately held her tongue. A smile and servile admiration lit up her disgusting face. As she excitedly counted the money with trembling hands, the minister and the Moroccan went out. They hurried down the stairs. The muffled sound of the distant kettledrum reached their ears. Then they once again heard the crying of a baby who could not be soothed. The Moroccan was in a good mood.

"There is a God, sir. That man died and was buried in a common grave in the paupers' section of the graveyard. And now somebody in Galatia will know when you write a letter."

"Take me back to the place where you picked me up," José said tersely.

4
Enemies of The Earthly Kingdom

"KEEP YOUR BUTTS LEVEL with the ground!" the group leader bellowed. "With the ground, I said!"

Dust filled the soldiers' nostrils. There was dust in their mouths, under their tongues, in their eyes. They crawled over the stunted thorny brush. There was just dusty dried earth everywhere full of sharp stones. Their hands were lacerated. Blood from the scratches on their faces mixed with sand and sweat had dried hard. Sand stuck to them on all sides. They crawled on breathing hard, their heads raised.

They stopped, waiting for a signal. Stretching before them was an area of open ground and an endless expanse of gray lifeless earth. Not a single tree or plant. The veins standing out on their necks, they lay pressed against the ground. Their ghostly faces were no longer recognizable.

Propped up on his elbows, Danilo grasped his rifle firmly. His eyes ran slowly over the wasteland in front of him. Then he lowered his head. Only a step away there was an anthill. Upturned red soil. He swore angrily to himself.

"I hope they don't make us dig in here!"

There were ants everywhere. They swarmed over the handle of the shovel, which, tied to his waist-belt, trailed on the ground. They crawled into trouser legs and sleeves. He didn't dare move. He shuddered at the thought that, while digging in a lying position, he had penetrated an anthill. He tried to move out of the way. No chance. It was as if all the insects in existence had gathered at this accursed spot. His uniform was torn. All the buttons were ripped off. From his open undershirt a chain with a pendant popped out swinging from side to side. For the umpteenth time, on the little brass tag he caught sight of his war number and the face of the emperor engraved inside the following inscription:

LORD, YOURS IS THE SKY
AND MINE THE EARTH

On top of a broken, scorched bush he spotted a grasshopper.

"Honestly, these creatures move around as if we didn't exist," he thought. "For crying out loud, don't let us dig in here!"

He recalled the old stories. Grasshoppers are holy creatures. They were made from the earth, just like man. And when man disappears, the grasshoppers will remain. That is why it is written in black Hebrew characters on the wings of grasshoppers: THE LORD IS ONE. He looked down again at his brass tag. YOURS IS THE SKY AND MINE THE EARTH. The insects seemed to be mocking him.

"For crying out loud, don't let us dig in here!"

There came a resounding bang. A signal rocket had been fired and was winging its way upward. Smoke trailed. A bright green flare appeared high in the sky.

"FOORRRWARD!!" shouted the group leader.

He was drowned out by the sound of the bugle.

"FOORRRWARD! For the emperor and your country!"

Several more incendiary flares exploded.

"CHAAAAARGE!"

With a terrible cry, the infantry streamed across the barren waste. A dense curtain of smoke descended. A gray cloud of dust rose from the ground under the feet of so many soldiers, it swirled and fused with the smoke. You couldn't breathe the air. You couldn't see a thing. The soldiers ran forward like madmen. They trampled on each other, suffocating in the dark smoke. The flame-throwers were spitting out fire. It was as if the fire would scorch earth, stone and men. The bugle sounded without respite. Salvos exploded on all sides.

"At the enemy!" the group leader thundered. "For the emperor and your country!

"CHAAAAARGE!"

The smell of newly-mown grass wafted up. Danilo lost consciousness. The image of green meadows melted into the unclear image of dead stone. In the stone sun-baked wilderness, the smell of grass spread.

"Poison gas!" screamed the group leader. "Poison gas! Get your masks out!"

Danilo thought he heard the sound of a bubbling brook. He tried to pull his gas mask over his face, but he didn't have the strength. He fell to his knees. Before him he saw fields of flowers. His nostrils flared, he faltered, he wanted to smell the fresh scent of colored petals. And the flowers, too, smelt of mown grass. He collapsed, hitting his head on the rock. He drifted into a sweet sleep, where he no longer felt any pain.

Soldiers fighting for their own lives passed the unconscious Danilo. They plunged forward crazily, over sharp rock they did not even see. Maddened, they rushed towards a way out of the smoke.

Far away, on an inaccessible elevation, a fat little general supervised the attack. Bareheaded, his hands behind his back, good-natured, he stood on a flat stone. His raised thick eyebrows and lined forehead could not disguise his satisfaction. A light breeze ruffled his thin white hair on an otherwise bald head.

Beside the general stood a tall, young major. In his new, immaculately ironed, well-fitting uniform, with a red band around his upper arm on the left sleeve, he looked dangerous, even though he was younger in rank. The major held up binoculars, clasping them firmly with both hands. The hands and binoculars completely masked his face, which had become coarse too early for his years. But the bright reflection of the sun showed the metal of the imperial cross and eagle on his cap.

"There's no war without infantry," the general remarked good-naturedly. "On terrain like this vehicles always get stuck. Even the cavalry can't get through the smoke. The horses get frightened. And just look at that thrust on the flank! That group leader has made excellent ground. What's his name?"

"Santillez, sir," replied the major, without lowering his binoculars.

"Well, he's good, that Santillez."

"Yes, he's good, sir. But he was given an easier line of advance."

"To a good officer all directions are equal."

"But if you would allow me, sir, to deploy the troops next time, that Santillez would not rush out so far. If he encountered just one large obstacle, he'd soon come a cropper."

The smile disappeared from the general's face. Without looking at the major he grudgingly conceded:

"Well, all right then. But take care that we don't lose too many men."

The major reached for his revolver. Barely concealing his glee and with a calm expression, he fired a yellow marker flare. Down in the pathless valley, this signal was observed by the officers. The shrill blast of a whistle rang out.

"Stop the attack! Cease fire!" the order sounded.

The bugles fell silent and the firing ceased.

"Cease fire!"

The soldiers fell to the ground.

There was silence. The breeze continued to blow, lifting the smoke-screen through which they had passed. The whipped up dust settled. Small particles of sand separated themselves from the smoke and gradually fell to earth. The song of crickets was heard, broken by a deep, muffled cough.

When the view cleared, it revealed the bodies of exhausted soldiers. They lay there, soundless, their gas masks covering their faces.

"Get up! Get up! Masks off!" roared Santillez, waving his arms. "Get up! They're watching us!"

The soldiers rose to their feet with great effort. Danilo alone, without a gas mask, stayed prostrate with bloodshot eyes. A bloody snot ran down a dirty cheek.

"He'll ruin everything!" the group leader shouted.

As he ran forward, he grabbed Danilo by the chest and shook him violently.

"Get up, you son of a bitch! You don't fool me! Get up! The gas isn't dangerous! This was an exercise!"

Danilo did not regain consciousness. The group leader unsheathed his knife. With one stroke he cut open Danilo's sleeve. He poured water from his flask over Danilo's swollen veins on the arms. Nothing helped.

Santillez was in despair that Danilo had fainted. This useless young man had ruined all his efforts regarding preparations for the exercise. Ruined all his hopes for promotion. If he had dared, he would have slit the youth's throat on the spot. He poured water over his face. Danilo didn't move.

"I'll kill you, you son of a bitch!" the group leader threatened. "You'll not get out of this alive, I promise you!"

He stamped on the outstretched arms of the unconscious young man with all the strength he could muster. His studded heels threatened to crush his fingers.

The major saw everything from the elevation through his binoculars. The old general, squinting in the sun, was following the overall disposition of the troops and was not interested in details.

5
I Can Touch You With My Hand

THE FIRST PART of the war exercise RESPONSE TO THE ENEMY had ended. Couriers were running about in all directions in the camp. The troops were seized with a feeling of apprehension. The felt that something was not quite right. Their foreboding was confirmed when they were given a sudden 24-hour furlough, which rarely happened in the border areas.

As they went out into the nearby town, the soldiers moved cautiously, always in a bunch of them. Only Santillez, ever a loner, separated from the others and went off somewhere on his own. The group leader was not afraid of the local population, which could never be trusted in these parts.

That evening the group leader found himself for the first time in a nightspot with dimmed red lights. He wore a new uniform and a clean shirt, which he had been issued just before he went out. He tried to conceal his depression. Due to Danilo's fainting fit, it was clear that he would not get his long-awaited promotion. As soon as he received his exit pass, he wanted to go out and get drunk and forget the misfortune that had befallen him.

Candles were burning on the table. In the dark room all you could see were parts of dark faces illuminated by the flame. Sitting at a table alone in a murky corner, the group leader sipped his strong red wine slowly, savoring every sip. He cast a threatening glance at the people around him. Filled with mistrust, he sensed danger. He clasped his revolver firmly with his right hand. He was prepared to kill the lot of them if he so much as noticed a suspicious movement. After he had downed several glasses, the group leader's mood improved. Surrounded by the smell of candle wax and wine, the group leader became increasingly calm. He relaxed, convinced that no danger impinged. He felt that no one was paying any attention to him. He even laughed at himself for his unnecessary caution. All the same, he kept his right hand in his pocket.

At one point the lights came on. Music started blaring out and the stage curtains parted. A tall, young woman took the stage. She had red hair and a silver crown on her head. She stood there, majestic, firmly clutching a shiny scepter under her pearl-sewn silk cloak. Surrounded by white smoke swirling out of the floor and lit by bright beams of green light, she looked every inch a queen. The spotlights were trained on her from all sides so she threw no shadow.

A loud announcement was interspersed with yearning sounds of the guitar in which her tender voice was mixed:

"*Adio...*"

She stood transfixed for a moment. Then she smiled, tossing aside her cloak and shiny scepter. Her white dress emphasized her slim waist.

"*Adio querida...*"

Santillez gave a start. It was in his language.

"*No quero la vida.
Me l'amargatest tu.*"

It was his language, but strangely changed. He did not know the song. He alone among these savages understood the incorrectly pronounced words. The beautiful woman seemed to be singing just for him.

Slowly the lights went down until only one dazzling spotlight remained on her. The shadow of the slim body was thrown against the wall. Everyone held their breath. Mouth agape, Santillez got up from his chair. He stood there frozen, half-erect, pushing himself up from the table with his palms. Her first lithe step forward changed into a sudden turn. Throwing back her head, she tossed aside the crown in her trance. The hidden musicians plucked their strings with ferocity.

"*Va, buxcate, otro amor...*"

In her struggle to maintain gravity, it was as though the tips of her toes barely touched the floor. As if her body was floating with outstretched arms. She tossed her head. Luxuriant unbound hair covered her face. Curls tied with silver ribbons shone under the strong light.

"*Aharva otra puertas,
Aspera otro ardor...*"

To the vibrant sound of the guitars she tapped her high heels on the floor. Crossing her hands on her chest, she closed her eyes and tossed back her head.

Then she opened her eyes.

Santillez stared at her open-mouthed, as if at a vision. For years he had not heard the sound of his native tongue and he still could not believe that he had heard it here in this hole at the end of the earth.

Another sharp tap and the jangle of bracelets.

"*Que para mi sos muerta...*"

The shadow of this lovely creature slid down from the wall. Then it stopped for a moment, and the sudden jerk, like a wave, ran from its knees, over smooth thighs and a trembling stomach, upwards all the way to its chest.

She noticed Santillez' awkward stance. Singing, smiling, she made her way towards the group leader's table.

"*Que para mi sos muerta!*"

Her outstretched left hand suddenly stopped in front of his face. The music grew soft. Spellbound, Santillez kissed the tips of her long white fingers, gripping them in his strong hand. She freed herself with a light movement. She caressed the stunned group leader very gently and tenderly on the neck.

Santillez failed to utter a word.

Lights flooded from all sides and the quivering shadow of the woman disappeared from the wall. A shower of colored confetti fell down from the ceiling.

Thunderous applause broke out from the guests. The music played loudly again. The mysterious singer backed gracefully to the spot where her cast-off crown lay. Conscious of her beauty, she waved to the admiring audience.

She knelt and adroitly picked up her fallen crown, then her scepter and cloak. She gave a smile and bowed elegantly, waving to the people lost in admiration. She tapped the scepter on the floor. At this sound, white smoke rushed up from the floor, wrapping itself around her. Hidden by the smoke, she exited the stage in the same way as she had entered it.

Other entertainers then performed — fire-eaters, clowns, ham-fisted magicians and dancers with flabby stomachs. Santillez didn't even notice them. He was furious with himself. In an absent moment, he had not summoned the courage to speak to her. It had only needed one word in his language. He simply had to find out who she was. He was sure that she liked him. Otherwise, why would she have stopped in front of him. He was pleased that he had put on his new uniform and taken a clean shirt for his day out.

He got up. At the exit he asked several of the waiters for her name. They shrugged their shoulders helplessly. One of them maintained she had no name, while another maintained she had forty secret names. They comforted him by saying that those bloody names were unpronounceable anyway and that no one on earth could remember them. They knew nothing else. He tipped them. They had said that the red-haired beauty was only passing through. They supposed that she had been exiled for some crime. He threatened them, cajoled them. He offered them more money, which they refused to take. They shook their heads dumbly.

Evening was approaching. The group leader had to get back to camp. He swore at the hapless waiters, he cursed army life and his own bad luck. The next exit pass would not be given for another week.

"I'll kill you, Danilo!" he swore. "I'll suck your blood! I'll murder you, you son of a bitch!"

His neck had swollen from rage. He unbuttoned his shirt collar to breathe more easily. Tired, he started to stumble, taking care not to trip. Bemused by the drink and the recent incident, he went to sleep it all off.

That night, the beautiful singer appeared in his dreams. But this time her face was covered with a black veil. Across the veil silver ribbons sparkled in place of her eyes. He woke up terrified. Still drowsy, he could not distinguish dream from reality. He was not even sure whether that woman was holding a silver scepter or whether her head was covered. But then he would not see her smile. He could not recall with clarity whether or not she was holding a scepter this time.

6
The First Woman

A Tale of the Sufferings of
Living Galatians and Dead Babylonians

IT WAS JUST PAST midnight when José returned to the State Administration Centre. The night guard looked at him in amazement.

"I forgot something." muttered the minister instead of a greeting.

The evening news came from the radio receiver at the reception desk.

"the general of the South Army and his colleagues attended part of an exercise over a wide area…"

José hurried towards his office. The voice of the announcer getting fainter, impersonal, almost inhuman followed him the length of the corridor:

"…a skirmish in which parts of assault units of the South-East military district participated as part of their regular military training. The war exercise **RESPONSE TO THE ENEMY** provided an opportunity to practice one of the possible methods of modern operations on our territory. On the spot on the ground, the general assured himself of the high degree of readiness of the military conscripts and rated this as excellent. At the end of the exercise, the general said: The time for negotiations has passed. We no longer have any faith in words."

Reaching his office, he slammed the door behind him.

"We no longer have any faith in words!" he smiled. "What is that exercise really like?"

He became depressed at the thought of the cruel conditions to which the soldiers were exposed. He was glad he didn't have anything to do with such events.

Unbuttoning his coat with one hand, he spread out the papers on the table with the other. He stared in consternation and the unusual letters. Then he searched through the pile once more. Except for that one sheet, all the others were written in a puzzling alphabet. He had never seen anything like it. In broken lines the Greek letters alpha, eta and ksi would appear, then the Hebrew dalet and kaf circled with dots. Many slanting crosses and flowers were mixed up with Ethiopian, Aramaic, Georgian, Arabic and who knows what other unknown characters. They repeated themselves in squares, circles, triangles, and triangles in circles. He began to make a list. After the first count, there were more than seventy different characters.

"What language is this?" the minister asked himself. "Is it written from right to left? Or vice versa?"

He tried to discern some familiar grammatical structures. Or at least some word that occurred more than once. But it was hopeless.

"We no longer have any faith in words!" — these words still rang in his ears.

"I can't resolve this tonight," he concluded grumpily.

He grabbed hold of the only sheet that was understandable.

"Dear brother Demetrakos, Phi, Kappa, Tau, Lilith... What could that mean?"

He moved to another desk where the computer stood. He typed the entry code and linked up with the Data-Processing Department. After he had keyed in three names, the following text appeared on the screen:

Demetrakos - not known.

ΦΚΤ - Phi, Kappa, Tau

Lilith - a female demon in Hebrew mythology. Corresponds to a witch in Serbia and Rumania. Her name also signifies a female evil spirit or the wind spirit in Assyrian and Babylonian lore. It was believed that Lilith had a particularly evil influence over children. This belief was also widespread among the Jews. According to their writings, Lilith was Adam's first wife. She was made from earth, at the same time as Adam, and not from a man's rib. Despite their identical origin, Lilith was in no way equal to Adam. She fled from the Garden of Eden, refusing to be subservient to Adam.

Surprised, José pressed the command to print. The machine whirred quietly and typed the text from the screen onto the paper.

"Strange!" he thought.

He was convinced that witches existed only in Galatia. And if there was an emperor of the Galatians in that benighted country, he could only be the master of evil forces.

In that country mothers watch over cradles at night to make sure their children do not smile in their sleep. For a happy smile is a sure sign that they have fallen victim to the charms of demons, who attract them with their beauty. Children die in their sleep and no doctor is able to find any trace of illness. Their only salvation is if their mothers wake them in time. Rescued from death at the last possible moment, these babies scream upon re-entering reality. Nothing, not their mother's embrace, nor all the love in the world can calm them down.

"Is it possible that Adam had a wife before Eve? A wife who refused to subjugate herself to him? There is nothing about that in official teachings. That's dangerous."

José took a form on which he left messages for his secretary. With quick strokes he wrote:

> *Urgent emergency meeting with the Minister of the Interior. Best time around ten, at his office in State Security. Later, a separate meeting with the principal of the School for Foreign Languages. Postpone all previously scheduled meetings.*

He folded the paper and put it in an envelope over which he poured red wax. He carefully pressed his ring into the soft wax. Then he wrote something on another sheet of paper and certified it with a large blue stamp. Once again he checked the text and put this paper in his briefcase.

He didn't notice the time passing. Deep in the night, just before the break of a new day, José hurriedly collected together all the papers from his desktop. He started off for a nearby hotel at a fast pace. He felt no fatigue. Far from it, he was very excited, clear-headed, and keen to start work. He didn't have time to go home. It was sunrise in no time and he knew that that he'd have to be rested for the latter half of that day. The unknown characters circled with dots danced before his eyes. The wavering dots pressed above the letters would vanish only to re-appear from the side, and later, double in number, below the characters.

His ears rang with the long-forgotten, incomprehensible refrain:

"Kamatz, kamatz katan, patach, kamatz, katan. We no longer have any faith in words!"
Something unreal was happening.

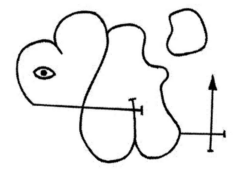

7
Unsigned Letters

THE WORKING DAY was well underway when José awoke. The sun's rays flooded the unfamiliar hotel room. José gave a start at the unpleasant thought that he was late for work. He remembered with relief that he had left a message for his secretary about canceling all previously scheduled meetings. The earliest obligation he had was at ten o'clock, the meeting with the Minister of the Interior. The clock on the bedside table said 9:12.

José got up quickly, showered and shaved. He buttoned his shirt and stood in front of the window which overlooked the square in front of the State Administration Centre. He gazed in confusion at the sidewalk where the cab had awaited him the night before. He couldn't stop thinking about the unexpected events. He got dressed and picked up his things. He set off deep in thought for the State Security building only a ten-minute walk away from the State Administration Centre.

José still found it difficult to go to State Security. Jets of water from the gaping jaws of two bronze dragons spouted in front of the huge white marble edifice. Stood facing each other, the monsters from the fountain inspired unease and foreboding in José. Arching high, the water jets burst into a cloud of tiny drops. Lit by the sun, the sparkling droplets bubbled in the air. As they fell, they lashed the surface of the dark water below. Cold waves splashed unceasingly against the stone pedestal in which the sharp dark green pointed tails of the dragons were embedded. The water bit into the stone and bronze, caressing them. At every moment it looked as though the sharp tails of the dragons would free themselves from the pedestal and disappear in the troubled water.

José went up to the fountain, staring at the water-splashed monsters. He stood there motionless, inhaling the fresh moist air floating above the water. He took out his pocket diary from his inside pocket and wrote:

Nothing in life happens by chance.
I will find those three young men!

"What are you doing there?" — he heard a raised voice.

"Looking at the water." José roused himself. He spotted a guard behind him.

"Looking and writing something down, huh?" — the guard thrust his face into José's, menacingly. He reeked of onion. "So, you think I'm the sort of man you can fool around with? Show me your papers!"

José uncomfortably balanced his briefcase under one arm, with his pocket diary and pen in his left hand, while his right hand drew out his pass.

The guard went pale. The duty officer, who had recognized the minister from a distance, was approaching them. With a click of his heels, the soldier stood to attention. Flushed with embarrassment, the officer wanted to bawl the man out, but José took him gently by the arm.

"What was he to do!" he soothed the officer. "I wouldn't let strangers wander round here either It's not written on a person's face who they are. Best if we keep this to ourselves. So they don't say afterwards that imperial officials are interfering with the army. Take me to Vicena."

José made towards the main entrance. The officer accompanied him. Although he had been upset at first, he soon calmed down, grateful that the misunderstanding would be kept under wraps.

They entered the building. Tearing out the page he had just written, José returned the diary to his pocket. He stopped on the staircase, one step behind the officer, and secretly ripped the page into four pieces. He took the unpleasant encounter with the guard as a mysterious warning.

"I must be more careful!" José thought. "I mustn't leave tracks!"

At some distance from them, the guard cursed his fate:

"Life's a fuck when a dwarf like that can ruin everything! It's a border post for me!"

Mr Vicena, the Minister of the Interior, greeted his visitor at the entrance to the main room. He was warm and smiling.

"Look you here! Who would've thought it?" — the man whom even the emperor feared grinned broadly. "What a pleasant surprise!"

"I have to admit that those dragons always upset me when I come to see you," José pointed through the window at the fountain.

"There you are, they have a calming effect on me! They symbolize all possible horrors. God's punishment for sinful mankind. Nothing's any good. There's absolutely no way of making people see reason! It seems that this unfortunate world begins at the exit from this building."

"I'm afraid that it's precisely because of a stroke of misfortune that I've had to come here myself!"

"What's happened, Alkorta, that necessitated such an urgent meeting? Is it possible that something escaped the notice of State Security? Unsigned letters?"

José gave a start. Surely they don't know everything already, he thought.

"They're not letters. It's not blackmail. I came here in connection with the University. The first students are due soon. I think there's going to be a flood of them."

"Well, we've only ourselves to blame when we promised them citizenship. OK, I would let them all finish their studies. But afterwards, it's 'Foreigners, get out of Rome!' Let them return to the backwoods where they came from!"

"There's no other choice! Nobody here expects Rome's own rich spoilt brats to learn anything. We need foreigners. And poor foreigners at that!"

José spoke carefully, slowly and clearly, taking care that no sudden shudder should cross Vicena's face. One wrong word could ruin everything. Even the right word, wrongly uttered. José spoke and smiled gently. His cheerful, penetrating, utterly trusting look lent force to his words. Vicena smiled, too. But the smile made Vicena's face ugly. José feared people who did not know how to smile. Which is why he was always on his guard with Vicena. Seeing that Vicena's attention was wandering, he became even more forceful.

"So we are expecting a flood of people. Especially from the outlying regions. Nonetheless, I intend to increase the number of medical students. So security is exceptionally important."

At the sound of this unpleasant word, Vicena raised his eyebrows. He was no longer smiling.

"What has security to do with medical students?"

"That's just the trouble. As soon as they become students, these young men can move anywhere they like. In Rome all doors will be open to them. The emperor himself will receive them."

"True. He's invested a lot of effort in this University."

"The best students will get a position at court. And, God forbid, that's a chance for deception, for robbery. I daren't even consider a greater misfortune, poisoning…"

Vicena was visibly annoyed.

"And what am I supposed to do?"

"It's imperative that a list be drawn up as soon as possible of all students who've applied. And each one of them must have someone to vouch for them."

"And who's supposed to do that?"

"Either you, or I. I don't see a third alternative."

"Listen, Alkorta! You're the minister for students!"

"Then you're the minister for poisoning!"

"Listen, Alkorta…"

"Or we can do it this way. You let me check out the students, and you take care of security. But I need special powers. I think thirty days is a long enough deadline."

José took out of his briefcase the sheet of paper with the big blue stamp.

"All I need is one signature."

Without a word, Vicena wrote his name and title with sharp strokes.

"I sense misfortune." José continued, returning the paper to his attaché case. "I don't want any unpleasantness now just before the University is officially founded. In any case I need a list of names of students with all their personal details."

Expecting an answer, José gave Vicena's shoulder a friendly pat.

The Minister of the Interior regained his good spirits. He shook José's hand for a long time.

"Don't worry about a thing. The list will be prepared by priority procedure."

As José was leaving, Vicena followed him with mistrustful eyes, looking through the parted curtains at the window.

"I think you kept something back, my friend! Poisoning?"

All the same, he could not help smiling through clenched teeth as he followed the clumsy walk of the skinny minister.

In his pocket José screwed up the four scraps of the torn page, which he had ripped out of his diary when he arrived. He wanted to destroy as soon as possible his own handwritten note about nothing in life happening by chance and about finding the three young men. He decided to throw them away in four different places so that no one could piece them together again. He knew that he must not make a single mistake. He had managed to extract special powers from Vicena giving him the unlimited right for the next thirty days to carry on activity in areas which were not in his remit. On the way out José was so deep in thought that he did not even notice that the guard who had asked him for his papers had already been replaced.

"I must find those three young men!" he thought, hurrying to the School for Foreign Languages.

8
The Infected Shirt

AFTER A BAD NIGHT, Santillez was washing in the morning when he noticed the skin on his neck was covered with tiny white spots. As he was still sleepy, he paid this no attention. The next day, the spots were bigger. He thought that he might have put on an infected shirt when he went out on his pass into town. Though the shirt he had been issued was clean and ironed. Now he cursed the unknown, infected soldier who had worn it before him. In desperation, he ripped off the collar and changed his underwear. He rubbed his neck with brandy and applied poultices of cabbage leaves but to no effect. The rash continued to spread each day, tormenting him with a painful itching. His skin looked as if it had been etched by acid.

9
New Future

The beginning of the story of a young man called Rinaldo

IF YOU SET OUT southwards from the town of Lutetia, an expanse of gentle hills rolls away as far as the eye can see. In one part there are thick woods, planted by the roadside itself. In summer, the entire area is green and luxuriant vegetation bursts into leaf like a living wall obscuring the view.

But winter devastates the surroundings. At such time, the outlines of guard towers in the valley can be discerned through the bare branches of the trees from a bend in the road. Round the towers rises a beautiful fortified stone wall as in ancient fairy tales. Only children and passing strangers pay any heed to the towers, which are visible during winter. Other people would try to keep as far away as possible. They do not even venture to look in the direction of the stone wall, which marks the boundary of NEW FUTURE, world of the damned.

In front of a metal door with an iron grille, a guard shoved the prisoner in roughly.

"Get in!"

Stepping into the prison courtyard, Rinaldo suddenly stopped terrified. A group of men were crouching round a puddle before him. With serious expressions and quick movements, they were exchanging pebbles. Not far from the puddle, one poor soul dressed in rags was crawling in the mud with a crazed look in his eyes. His palms and knees were covered with a thick layer of calluses.

"God almighty! Where have they brought me?"

Behind him he heard the squeak of rusty locks and the clang of the door closing. The men crouching on the ground, rinsed the pebbles in the puddle and passed them to each other, ignoring the newcomer. Giving them a wide berth, Rinaldo continued to walk along the edge of the wall. Only one man in the gloomy courtyard smiled. Pleased with himself, he was collecting fallen leaves from the mud with a rake. In a world of his own, he worked on staring at the mud and nothing else interested him.

The yard was spacious and surrounded on all sides by a tall stone building. From outside the prison looked like a fortress, into which a building had been erected from the inside containing the cells. The windows on the upper floors were barred. At the far end there were no windows or bars, just a bare wall on which were written the words:

**HE WHO OBEYS THE RULES
SHALL HAVE ETERNAL LIFE.**

"Good! So it is a prison!" he gave a sigh of relief.

He calmed himself as he realized that he was in prison, not a madhouse. They don't write messages on the walls of madhouses. However deceptive or ridiculous the words, at least in their written form they are man's pride and joy.

"So it is a prison!" he convinced himself, much calmer now.

The prisoners knew that Abaddon monitored every step the young man took. Abaddon was everywhere and at all times. They did not dare utter his name. The warden had only appeared to his prisoners once, on the occasion of serious riots. He had tied a knout with lead balls on the leather thongs to his left hand. Rumor had it that once, in a fit of fury, he had cracked open the head of some unfortunate with one blow from his fist. That story was probably invented, but it had enough truth in it for every argument to cease whenever Abaddon appeared in the distance. The tale went that his nostrils were as wide as those of an animal, that his face was twisted, and that mucous poured out of the sides of his mouth. Some maintained that his left eye was blue and the right one black. The very thought that Abaddon was a man at all seemed improbable, and, as a consequence, that he would one day die. People who have always enjoyed freedom cannot conceive of the immortality the downtrodden attribute to their persecutor. In the world of men stripped of their rights, everyone appears stupid. Both those whom nature has punished and those whom she has endowed. So it was not known who was truly mad, and who feigned madness.

Even in the prison not all men were equal. For while some languished in chains in cellars, others could look at the sun and the blue sky.

Rinaldo sat down on a wooden bench beside the wall. The muddy yard was crisscrossed with paved walkways. Where the paths crossed there were blue swans made out of rubber and wire as decorations. At the far end of the yard seven birches grew. Gentle, noble trees, which looked as if they had been planted in the prison by mistake. Their branches reached upwards towards the sun and freedom.

From a first-floor window through parted curtains, the warden of New Future followed Rinaldo with his eyes.

"I don't like this guy one single bit." Abaddon mumbled.

"He's strong, this idler!" the head of the reform service smiled. "But he'll soften up soon, Warden!"

Abaddon peeked through the curtain without turning round.

"He's already soft. There's something cursed about him! Some evil!"

10
The Leaves Of The Wind

THE SIGNAL FOR EVENING filled the corridors of New Future. Outside, in the deserted courtyard, the whistle indicating night was lost in the gusts of autumn wind which bore the fallen, dry leaves. Darkness spread in the lower parts of the building. A ghostly light burned only in the warden's first-floor room. Through the opaque, misted glass the vague outline of a man was visible, a man of heavy step burdened with worry.

The light from the window fell upon the bare branches of the birches. Their shadows bent this way and that under the onslaught of the wind and were lost in the dark ground.

Abaddon searched through the official report in vain. The carefully collected Statements of informers and the incomplete official data revealed only part of the truth about Rinaldo.

Rinaldo was born after the death of his father. And his mother died giving birth to him. Left an orphan, he grew up with his grandfather. Already as a child, he distinguished himself by his strength. He soon proved to be superior in fencing and fast riding. There was no one to touch him in the whole of Catalonia. As a young man he had taken part in war campaigns. With his great strength, he could wrestle a horse and its rider to the ground. Just as it was expected that Rinaldo would join the imperial cavalry, he took a fall from his horse for some insignificant reason and was badly injured. It was thought he would become a cripple for life and that his right leg would always be shorter. Later he got a fever. The young man lost consciousness and was shaking. For days, running a cold sweat, he screamed with pain. But his screams were not in Catalonian. When the pains subsided, Rinaldo remained delirious, not regaining consciousness. He seemed to be obsessed with some unclean power that wanted to kill him in this mad state.

It was precisely at this point that by chance two dark-skinned strangers rode into their area. With limpid pale green eyes and frizzy hair, dusty from the long journey, their very appearance was enough to scare the dark-eyed local peasants. Everything about them was strange: the trappings on their horses, and their tall boots, and their curved double-edged swords. The suspicious peasants did not dare drive the strangers out. Instead, they retired fearfully inside their houses. They were filled with dread as soon as they thought of the way the older stranger who never said a word looked. Apprehension about this man spread. Anyone who happened to come across him felt his heart freeze. The strangers stayed all the time on the main road, long expecting someone to approach them. After some time there appeared the village hunchback, whose mind was disturbed. He ran up to the strangers, waving his hands and beating his forehead. As he came up to the older rider's horse, he suddenly got scared of the decorative star, which gleamed on the animal's headpiece. Bowing and muttering incomprehensibly, he led the strangers to the house of Rinaldo's grandfather.

The strangers spoke to each other in a language that no one knew. It was only when they dismounted that the younger one said something understandable as he unpacked the saddlebag:

"Sickness doesn't come from outside. It comes from inside, from man himself!"

The weather was hot. They carried the sick man's bed out into the yard. The older stranger took a bunch of dried prickly leaves and waved it for some time over the sick man's head. His lips moved, but the rustling of the leaves prevented you from knowing whether he was muttering something or singing.

"That's the leaves of the wind rustling," explained his assistant.

At the end of the long waving, the stranger kissed Rinaldo on the forehead, as if trying to suck up the illness with this kiss. As he lifted his head, he spat to one side. For days the strangers pounded some knotty roots with a stone. The hunchback who had shown them the way never stopped weeping.

"Forgive me, Lord!" came the cry of the poor wretch as he kissed the tracks of the horses' hooves in the dust.

In a pot the strangers boiled a mash from the medicinal roots and long-bladed leaves that the peasants had never seen before in their woods. During all this time, the village children were kept shut in their homes so that no evil from the mysterious strangers could harm them. After a long healing period, the strangers managed to mend the fracture with their bitter ointments and their splints. The leg was now the same length as before the fall.

Thus Rinaldo recovered through a miracle. And everything seemed the same as before that fateful day. But his nature had changed. He never again touched his military weapons, but turned instead to studying books. All his previous friends started avoiding him, saying that Rinaldo had become treacherous and harbored some evil intent. Rejected by his fellow men, Rinaldo fell in love with foreign languages and ancient shabby books. These books became his only friends. It was obvious to everyone that the miracle-workers had cast a spell over him. The story went that Rinaldo was studying diabolical languages, in which he had cried out in his sick delirium.

Forty days after the arrival of the strangers, another misfortune occurred. Three little girls died in the village, one after the other. A terrible curse fell upon the healers, and hence Rinaldo, too. A blind woman, a fortune-teller, swore that Rinaldo, although already quite strong again, had also drunk the lives of the three hapless little girls and so become invincible. People believed these incredible stories even though Rinaldo was incapable of fighting after his fall. Life had become impossible for him in his native land.

He wanted to go to Rome. Earlier he had written several applications to be accepted at the School for Foreign Languages. He never had a reply. Rinaldo lost hope and went to Lutetia, a town which, at the timer, was much smaller and less important than imperial Rome. He disappeared without trace. All that reached Catalonia was the odd rumor that Rinaldo was living with some woman, a painter. It was said that he constantly studied books and that his face had grown deformed through reading, so much so that he was barely recognizable. After this, nothing more was heard about him. And in time, people stopped even mentioning him.

In the town of Lutetia, Rinaldo earned a living by translating books of national importance. He would probably have lived out his life in peace if his landlord had not wanted to get rid of him. The law on renting out apartments protected Rinaldo so his landlord reported him to the office for public security. Untroubled by this, Rinaldo expected that the disagreement would be resolved as soon as the matter reached some higher-ranking investigator who would easily understand his situation. However, he was interrogated by men who every day had to deal with murderers, whores and burglars and who detested suspicious characters like Rinaldo. So without any explanation, Rinaldo was taken to New Future.

11
A Dog's Death

"GET A MOVE ON! Faster!" shouted the warder. "Move those shoulders!"

Naked to the waist, the prisoners walked round the yard on the compulsory evening exercise. A cold wind was blowing.

New Future was a world from which nobody went anywhere. Even the warders never got an official transfer, but ended their lives in the same place as their prisoners. Every man is condemned to life imprisonment.

The prison cells and corridors were filled with unhealthy damp air and constant darkness. That is why the prisoners looked forward to every chance to get into the prison yard. Rinaldo alone walked in a dejected manner, his face tense. Once again he felt a pain in his leg, in the same spot where he had once fractured it. Apart from the old aches, he now had pains in his joints from the cold. It appeared he would end his days in the prison damp. He rubbed his hands together to try and alleviate the pain and warm his frozen fingers. At every step he took, a sharp pain flashed through his right leg. He limped along trying to avoid the water, which had filled the yard as a result of the long rains. His worn out prison shoes were wet.

"Been here long, lad?" — he heard a screeching voice behind him.

He turned. Petrified, he saw beside him the man with whom nobody was supposed to talk. It was the first time Rinaldo had seen him close up. The wrinkled old man with curly gray hair was trying to smile. His half-open mouth revealed decayed teeth. The rotting stumps made Rinaldo feel sick. He had the impression everyone was looking at the two of them. He realized that the prisoners would kill him if he broke the rule, so Rinaldo mumbled something, inwardly cursing his bad luck. He turned back and tried to move away from the old man.

"Well, it's been twelve years since they brought me here" — he heard the same voice behind him.

"What's twelve years?" he replied unwillingly. "Being tortured by your conscience is a greater punishment than wasted time. And you yourself know it's better if we don't talk."

"I didn't do what they sentenced me for."

Rinaldo looked at him without speaking. The old man started to cry. "I didn't assault my daughter! I didn't poison my son!" — his bony arms flailed.

The old man with broken health, was answering for crimes for which there is no forgiveness even for the cruelest murderers and outlaws. Criminals who had killed dozens of people considered that raping your own daughter was the worst crime of all.

"Where're you from?" Rinaldo asked him.

"From Colchida."

"From Colchida?" he said in surprise.

He noticed only now that the old man had unusually light-colored eyes.

"Yes, from Colchida." — the old man calmed himself. -"Do you know where Colchida is?"

"Yes" Rinaldo smiled, thinking of the two men who had saved him. "Actually, I've always wanted to travel round your country."

They stopped for a moment, and then carried on talking as they walked.

"Things haven't been good there for years. I hear they are now arresting people for nothing. The time has come when honest people are in jail, and criminals are out on the loose. That's why you're safest in jail. But do you know what freedom is, my son?"

Rinaldo reflected for a moment. He inadvertently glanced at the writing on the wall. HE WHO OBEYS THE RULES SHALL HAVE ETERNAL LIFE. He recalled answers learned long ago. People live in a state of dependence, incapable of attaining the world of freedom. A world without any restrictions. He felt uneasy as he was aware that the old man wouldn't understand any explanation of such a complex notion as freedom.

"And how do you know what freedom is?" asked Rinaldo, evading an answer.

"I am the chosen one!" The old man's eyes bulged and he let out throaty sounds as if choking. "I have been chosen to save the world!"

With all the strength left in his twisted body he endeavored to convince the young man.

"What is freedom?" Rinaldo asked soothingly.

"See here, son, freedom is the basis of life. Without freedom, there is no life."

The swollen veins on his neck relaxed and his gullet stopped shaking. Having rid himself of some dark force, it seemed, the old man continued:

"No animal can live cooped up. Any animal, if closed in, goes peculiar. It loses its strength, and stops reproducing. Freedom is as necessary as water, food and the sun. Even a bird can't live in a cage. An eagle has to be free. It only builds its nest on cliffs. And in order to spread its wings, its needs space. It's a sin to put an eagle in a cage. And it's a real deception to see an eagle on the imperial flag. All the empire has left now is space. And they lie when they say we have freedom!"

Rinaldo listened to all this in amazement. For a moment he got the impression that the old man's voice had changed, that somebody else was speaking from his body.

"Why are you here?" Rinaldo asked.

"Because of my son. He got himself mixed up in affairs of state. They took him off for questioning. Held him for a month. When he came home, he had faded like an old woman. We scarcely recognized him. He kept throwing up, day after day. At the end of a week, he died. His breath just froze. Next day the registrar came and recorded death from natural causes."

"But what did your son die of?"

"A dog's death, you can be sure."

"A dog's death?"

"When you swallow that, you're a goner," his voice trembled. "They used to force undesirables to drink oxblood. They died on the spot. But then they had to enter them into the registers as poisoned. Now they let you home. And that dog's death chokes you for a whole week. You're alive, but you're retching all the time. Until death gobbles you up. Then the registrar comes. He explains that he has to know the details of every deceased person. Everything has to be written down. But what do they need state registers for, when there are no honest people. And I have no son."

Tears welled up in the old man's eyes. His lower jaw started to quiver. "They accused me falsely just so as nobody could find it in their heart to come near me!" he sobbed. "Just so that nobody would find out the truth here either!"

That evening Rinaldo could not get to sleep for a long time. Up to then they had taught him that animals were not free because they were not governed by reason but by their instincts. He covered himself with the dirty blanket and turned his face to the wall. Damp was visible at the joins of the stone blocks. He knew that he must not turn with his back to the wall otherwise he would be howling in agony the next day. As always, he slept in a semi-stiff position at the very edge of the bed. His bed of boards was chained to the cold wall. He could not get away from the wall.

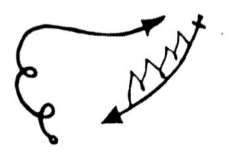

12
Preparation For Death

AFTER HIS ENCOUNTER with the old man Rinaldo had a strange dream. He saw himself climbing a broad circular staircase with great effort.

He was in a building whose interior he did not recognize. In front of him he saw an empty, closed space with the circular staircase in the middle. At first, he walked slowly, prepared for a long climb. The staircase gradually narrowed. His legs felt increasingly heavy. His movements became slower. He was losing his strength. The incline grew steeper and steeper. He clung desperately to the handrail and hauled his tired body up. He began to feel dizzy. He could no longer think. He had the feeling that he would die on this endless staircase. And just as the last ounce of strength was deserting him, he saw a plaque to which the staircase led. He caught sight of a great space on this floor, but the walls were lost in mist and he couldn't see them. Faltering, gasping for breath, he managed to reach the last step. He succeeded in throwing himself up onto the floor block. He had no sooner dragged himself there than there was a sudden crash. The staircase collapsed. He sat there, pressing his hands down onto the floor so that he would not tumble down himself. Marooned above the abyss, he sat on the edge of the floor to which nothing led any more. He turned around. Through thick mist he saw misty scenes and lightning flashes. Then, as in a mirror, there appeared a clear picture of the roofs of a large city. He saw a pigeon fluttering its wings and taking off high into the sky. Not far from the city, above the coast, two hawks swooped down on the pigeon. And just as it looked as though the hawks would tear the weaker bird to pieces, the scavengers suddenly attacked each other. They fought to the death, ripping out feathers with bloodied claws and beaks. In the meantime, the pigeon flew off. The vision faded as if the lead and pewter back of the mirror was melting away.

A toothless old man appeared with fiery blue eyes, long white hair and a white beard. He was holding a silver cane in his hand. "I have come to talk to you," he said. "Do not despair! I have come to prepare you for death!"

Horrified, Rinaldo woke up with a start. Half-conscious, he realized that he was sitting up. He was pressing his hands down on the side of the bed, while his legs were dangling above the floor. The dirty bare light bulb threw an irritating yellow light. His eyelids were stiff with pain. After his conversation with the old man, he had the impression that the other prisoners were now following his every movement, even in the night. Water was dripping from the ceiling. From the adjoining cell came the rasping cough of someone with sick lungs. The cough changed to a fit of choking and gurgling like a death throe. On the other side, someone gave a long fart. There was still a lot of time before daybreak.

13
Mathematics Is Music

This is a recollection of two Jews who grew up among the Galatians and later moved to a distant country where the Galatians do not live. They became leading military commanders and met again for the first time in wars for their new homeland. In the midst of campaigns, they communicated with each other in a language from their childhood, which neither their friends not their enemies could understand. The two generals dreamed in Galatian.

In reality, their dreams were stronger than listening devices.

THE PRINCIPAL OF the School for Foreign Languages received José in his office. He was already gray-haired, a professor of dignified bearing. He wore glasses with thick lenses. Concealing his excitement, he extended his hand to his distinguished visitor.

"Minister, I expect you've come about the school being abolished."

"To be honest, your school does not have a bright future. The empire needs physicians, not language teachers. But that's not why I'm here."

After this discouraging reply, the principal no longer questioned the reason for this important man's visit:

"What interests me is whether there are artificial languages."

"You mean computer languages?"

"No, I mean spoken languages."

The professor raised his eyebrows.

"Something that could be used for a secret correspondence inside the ministry," José explained.

"Well, there's Esperanto."

"Yes. But that's a mixture of already existing languages. Are there, for example, languages for written, but not spoken communication?"

"The languages of dead peoples! They can be read, but no one knows how most of these languages were pronounced."

"Is that all?"

"No! There are so-called mathematical languages. You see, while the two of us are talking, we are using grammatical rules we're not even aware of. These rules only become apparent when we use a foreign language. All that we are saying now can be written using a sign or a number. For example, if you talk in Catalan, someone can transcribe what you say into mathematical signs. Later these signs can be re-translated into any language spoken in the empire."

José felt uncomfortable.

Noticing that his visitor was carefully listening to his words, the professor continued his explanation enthusiastically:

"And not only language! Drawing conclusions, too. Human thought. This can all be done through mathematical logic. When drawing conclusions, there are always basic assumptions. These assumptions can be written down on paper in the form of mathematical signs. If you apply to this writing certain mathematical rules, you will obtain new different signs. And these signs, translated back into human language represent the conclusion you would have reached through your own consideration."

"So, mathematicians know models of human thought? The minister expressed his surprise."

The professor was visibly excited:

"Not only human! Not only human! Human reasoning is only one of the countless models known to mathematics. And in its way, the simplest! And how many other things are there in the heavens and on this earth our knowledge can only guess at. The world which we perceive with our senses is unbearably simple. Among men, only mathematicians have an inkling of other, to us unknown, worlds."

"You mean, logic?"

"I mean everything! For example, we see mostly in three dimensions. Mathematicians find it easy to find their way in space with many more dimensions. In our world it seems to be true that parallel lines do not intersect. However, there are worlds in which those same parallel lines do intersect. There exist problems in our world that cannot be solved. By applying rules like Laplace or Fourrier's transformations especially, these problems can be transferred, in a changed form, into another world where they are easy to solve. Then, the reverse rule is applied to solutions that are not as yet understood. And so here we are, back in our world, with a solution that can be understood. At the point from which we started. But the simple human mind is incapable of imagining this."

José could not believe that incomprehensible writings could be represented by some mathematical equation. Up to then he had been convinced that everything was just a translation of something understandable, which had in some way been hidden. Now he felt discouraged, but he continued to listen to the professor.

"Take music, minister! Music is part of mathematics, too. Every sound, every beat. Everything is mathematics."

This was the final blow. José slowly got to his feet.

"Professor, you've been a great help."

"It was a great honor."

"As far as your staff is concerned, we shall probably transfer most of them to the state service. In any case, no decision has been taken yet."

"That's a pity, minister. A great pity. Our students are very talented. We are well-known throughout the empire. You should just see the sort of young men we have to turn down."

He picked up a letter from his desk and handed it to the minister. José ran his eyes over the contents. It was an enrolment application for the school.

"This boy speaks twelve languages" — the professor interrupted him

José looked down the list. One of the languages was Galatian.

"Good God!" he thought. "How on earth do these letters get to me. I wonder if it's a trick. That taxi driver could have been a plant. Yet, I came to see this professor of my own will. Moreover, the taxi driver didn't know where I was from. This is incredible!"

The young man's name was Rinaldo. He said in his application that he also knew how to make up medicines. This knowledge could be useful in getting into medical school. They were going to abolish the language school in any case. If Rinaldo were to come to Rome, a way could be found to get him to translate the writings. The minister had the feeling that Rinaldo was talented. If he wasn't, he wouldn't have sent the application.

"In addition, this young man is also a Roman citizen" — the professor's voice once again broke in.

"Then accept him."

"But there are problems. This Rinaldo is currently in prison. He's done nothing wrong. It was just a false report. Envy on someone's part. Who can tell? Anyway, it must be clear to you what it means to be shut up in New Future."

"Professor, please allow me to keep the letter. There are too few of our own citizens applying for enrolment. I'll see if something can't be done."

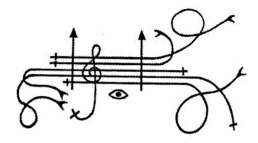

14
Life Is A Dream

AS HE LEFT the school, José thought about how to free Rinaldo from prison. He would have to think up some false order which would not be filed anywhere. An order that would leave no trail.

"It's a strange day today," said Federico as they neared the State Administration Centre. "There's never been a rush quite like it, from one end of the city to the other."

"Yes. I'm really tired," replied the minister, giving the driver a wink. "I've already got a headache."

"And I can barely keep my eyes open," said Federico, nodding. He sensed that something important was afoot.

"I've just got a few details to look at in the office. But I should take a walk in the fresh air until my headache goes. Would you like to join me, Federico?"

"Of course, minister. Nothing easier."

"Wait for me in the car. I'll be right back!"

He ran into the building, jumping up the stairs two at a time. Breathless, he wiped his forehead with his handkerchief. His secretary was waiting for him in front of his office with a sheaf of work orders in her hand.

"Tomorrow! Let everything wait till tomorrow! I'm too busy today!"

Forcing a smile, he was trying to get rid of her as soon as possible. He stepped backwards, his face turned towards the woman, then entered the room and closed the door. Without even bothering to take off his coat or sit down at his desk, he typed one name into the computer. At great speed, one after the other, the following glittering letters appeared on the dark screen:

As a result of an oversight in the investigation procedure, as a captain, Mr. Karamark was mistakenly sentenced to death for treason. After the statements of witnesses were checked, he was exonerated from the charge, but stripped of his rank. Currently he is on the **Response to the Enemy** *exercise with the rank of major. He is preparing to sit an exam for the rank of lieutenant-colonel.*

José took the little silk flag from the desk. With a deft movement he untied the ribbon from the support. He spread it out between his fingers and looked at the embroidered red rose inside the six-pointed yellow star. Then he put the ribbon in his pocket.

"A whole train of strange coincidences is following me." He recalled the midnight news — **Response to the Enemy** war exercise.

He pressed a key and erased the text from the screen. He walked quickly towards the exit from the building.

As they were driving, those letters seemed to haunt him as if in a dream:

"...kamatz, kamatz, katan, patah, kamatz, katan. We no longer have any faith in words!"

Since the day the cab driver had unearthed his secret, José's life had been a nightmare. Everything looked as if it was somehow linked, every detail, every word. He felt that he only had to follow the events that succeeded one another. But as soon as he tried to find a connection, all the events melted into each other as in a dream, which you forget upon waking. His own conclusions would then appear to him too simple and worthless. He was ashamed of his naivety and the time wasted. And this disappointment would last until he once again caught sight of the discovered writings and his own notes. This was irrefutable proof which once more transported him into an unreal world in which he got lost yet again.

Federico stopped the car near the walkway by the river. José got out and looked around him to check whether anyone was trailing them. The promenade was deserted.

The minister and the driver walked slowly and talked about the cloudy weather. Federico was confused. When they got to a fountain, José's voice suddenly changed.

"Now we can talk. Splashing water is the best defense against eavesdropping."

"Minister, is everything all right?"

"Federico, would you be prepared to do something for me?"

"Minister, do you even doubt that?"

"This is very important!"

"But, minister, you saved my life!"

"You could lose your head over this!"

"If it hadn't been for you, I'd no longer be among the living. Not me, not that major. I always remember that whenever I look at the ribbon on your desk."

"Do you know that major?"

"I know him by sight. But he doesn't know me."

"You'll soon have an opportunity to see him again!" José's eyes flashed.

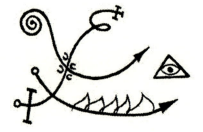

15
False Bottom

ALL DECISIONS OF SIGNIFICANCE for the life of the great empire were taken in Rome. One of the major tasks of the State Security service was to transmit messages and orders from the city of Rome, unchanged and to the furthest corners of the empire. Beneath the ground a network of telephone, electric and computer cables had been dug. Above ground messages were sent via radio waves and signals. The people from State Security monitored every spoken word; nothing could be hidden from them.

While informers took care of the easily identifiable things, only an idle old man on the main square noticed the strange pigeon that soared up into the sky and headed southwards.

"There are pigeons and pigeons," he said to his friends in the inn. "But I've never seen one like that. It's a real carrier. They only used them in the army. And, God knows how long ago that was!"

In the military pigeon station in the southern wastelands, the soldier on duty was bored. Nothing had happened for months. In any case, he only did his duty and never asked himself why they used such an old-fashioned method of sending messages. He learned a long time ago that in the army it was best to think as little as possible.

Desert clouds sailed high above the dead coastline. Squashed flat, they looked like a transparent line whose edges were shrouded in foaming damp whirlpools. His senses blunted by boredom, the soldier lazily examined the clouds and the endless sky. Suddenly, he spotted a white bird in the sky. He gave a start. Although the ocean was not far off, seagulls were a rare sight. And the seagulls in that area were black. He rubbed his eyes in amazement. It was a pigeon. A real pigeon!

When the bird landed, the soldier was surprised to see that the metal ring on its leg was tied with some kind of ribbon. He untied it and saw a six-pointed yellow star inside framing an embroidered red rose with six petals. He wanted to throw it away, but then he saw the name of Major Karamark engraved on the metal ring. The very thought of this man scared him. He decided that it was better to take the bird, the ribbon and the ring to him straight away.

Major Karamark, unusually clean and neat for that wilderness, immediately dismissed the soldier from his presence. He stood beside a tent, facing north-west. The slowly floating clouds fused into a heavy motionless one. A storm was brewing. Staring at the endless stony desert before him, he rubbed over the embroidered ribbon between his fingers. Then he set it alight with a flame from his lighter.

"So, you've found me!" he murmured. "One good turn deserves another! Let it all end now!"

From then on, he went regularly to the pigeon station. He inquired about any new messages, but no more came. He knew that Alkorta left nothing to chance and that a new message would soon arrive. The ribbon was just a sign that he should be ready. The soldier at the pigeon station realized that something important was underway. He stared into the sky incessantly. But to no avail. The major came to check and got more and more depressed. The days passed and nothing happened. The major decided to go to the nearest town. He wanted to make sure that perhaps some regular message had not arrived in the meantime.

The jeep stopped in front of the post office, raising a cloud of dust. The major stepped smartly towards the entrance. He caught sight of a beggar on the stone step. His hair matted and tangled and covered with ash, he looked a sadder sight than any beggar he'd ever seen. So poor that he didn't even have any clothes but covered himself with a coarse blanket. It seemed all he had in the world was the dented tin begging plate.

"There's no limit to human misery," thought the major.

From his pocket he took out a copper coin and gave it to the beggar. At that same moment, the major was aghast to see reflected in the plate a painted image of a red rose inside a six-pointed yellow star.

"Who are you?" he asked the unfortunate.

"I am sent by the great Lord," answered the beggar, without lifting his head.

"Have you got something to give me?"

"Only this!"

He held the plate with both hands. Stooping, the major grabbed the beggar by the elbow with all his strength. With the other hand, his grip tightened on his pistol.

"Get up, you cur! On your feet!"

Two soldiers leapt out of the jeep, their weapons at the ready. Curious passers-by turned to look at them. Grasping the beggar firmly, the major led him to a side entrance to the post office. He gave the door a sudden kick. The ancient lock immediately gave way. He shoved the beggar into a dark, smelly corridor. The soldiers remained outside in the street as protection, ready for any emergency. Inside, at the other end of the corridor, the major looked into the eyes of a woman, glowing like two coals in the dark.

"Get out of here!" he shouted. "Beat it!"

She did not move. The major shuddered as if he was seeing the devil himself. He aimed the pistol in her direction. The eyes vanished. From far off he heard pleading in a language he did not understand.

The major turned towards the stranger:

"Talk!"

The beggar held out the plate.

"Inside is a letter. Send a man to Lutetia. The letter must be handed to the people in charge of the New Future prison. It must not go via Rome, but by a roundabout route. As soon as he finishes this, let him go. He must not return to the army. It's too dangerous."

Fateful female curses rang out, mixed with very clear Roman oaths. The major tucked the plate under his shirt. He gave a nod:

"Off you go!"

When they went out into the main street, the major pushed the beggar away from him so roughly that the man fell on his face.

"Beat it, you thieving cur!"

People had started to gather. The dirty children had stopped making a din. Hunched old women, their heads tied round with black scarves, were whispering to each other. Any threatening movement was followed closely by the eyes unshaved men. All of a sudden, an old woman threw a handful of rice in front of the officer. Ignoring this challenge and completely in control, the major moved away. The soldiers jumped into the jeep. Raising himself from the ground, his dusty face now streaked with flowing blood, the beggar went shakily on his way.

No one noticed that his plate was missing.

In a hurry to return, the major himself drove. Throwing rice was a sign of welcome in those parts. All the same, the major didn't give a damn whether, this time, this gesture could have meant something else. His thoughts were fixed on the plate.

When they arrived in camp, he went to his tent. He broke the tin plate open with a hammer and chisel. In the hidden compartment of the false bottom, he found a sealed letter with an imprinted certification.

"Why is he dragging me into all this?" he wondered, turning the letter over in his hand. "The certifications are false. Even so, that beggar could have got to Lutetia himself, just as he got this far. It seems the letter must be delivered by someone in uniform. So those people in the prison don't suspect. But who?"

He grabbed the telephone.

"Captain!"

"Yes, major!" came the sleepy voice from the earpiece.

"Captain, what was the name of that dozy soldier who passed out?"

"Just a minute, major, let me check."

For a long time nothing was heard. Then the same voice came back on the phone, but far more decisive this time.

"Danilo. Danilo, major. His name is Danilo."

"Bring him here at once!"

"You're right, sir! Men like him deserve to be punished!"

The major put down the receiver.

16
The Morning Hours Have Golden Mouths

A HOT DRY WIND had been blowing for days without respite. When it gusted, it sucked up whole clouds of dust from the stony land. With heads bowed, the soldiers put up barbed wire obstacles. The sound of striking picks and heavy mallets echoed. The soldiers' hands were bloody as they knocked steel pegs into the stone. At the top of the cliff the wind whipped the blue flag with the cross and eagle which had been driven into the rock. The soldiers could hardly move their legs for fatigue. They seemed to be chained to the spot under the weight of their steel-studded boots. Every time they moved on they had carefully to lift their weapons, wrapped in canvas for protection, from the rocks and put them down again close to hand. For they knew that not far away the enemy's flag fluttered, with its lion and sun symbols.

They were in no man's land, between the two borders. A cursed area with hot days and unbearably cold nights.

"It's a good job a man doesn't know in advance what awaits him!" someone was grumbling. "If I'd known, I'd rather have killed myself that let them bring me here."

Danilo could barely hold the mallet in his lacerated hands. At night his skin split from the cold. Blood ran from his fingertips, which his illness had caused to appear as if they'd been cut into with a knife. During the day the unhealed wounds would be subject to further wounding from the barbed wire.

"I'll kill him!" Santillez was watching Danilo with hate-filled eyes. "It's his fault we were sent here!"

Sensing danger, Danilo turned round towards the group leader. He had long felt that Santillez would kill him. Maybe that very evening while he was asleep. He looked at his enemy. He was surprised to notice that the group leader's face was an unhealthy yellow and his forehead covered with dark spots. The wind ruffled his matted sand-filled locks. His open shirt revealed damaged skin on the neck. The tissue was dead.

"What are you staring at?" Santillez yelled.

With his left hand he nervously buttoned up his collar.

"Nothing!" Danilo mumbled, lowering his gaze.

"How dare you answer back!" Santillez kept his hands on his belt. His fingers were trembling. "You insult an officer! You insult a Roman officer!"

The rest of the soldiers stopped their work, scared stiff.

"You're all witnesses!" Santillez roared. "You all saw what the traitor did!"

Suddenly from the distance came the sound of a horn. The soldiers grabbed their weapons and threw themselves flat behind the shelter. They forgot all about Danilo. On his stomach with his head slightly raised, Santillez stared into the wilderness before him. His left hand shaded his eyes from the sun and the dust. The lookouts reported that a vehicle was approaching.

"It's ours!" shouted Santillez, recognizing the markings on the jeep. "Belts! Belt up! On the double! Get on with your work! As if nothing had happened."

Spellbound, he peered in the direction the vehicle was coming from. His mouth broadened into a stupid grin. He had hoped that his superiors had finally taken note of his efforts. He had long awaited a decree on promotion. It was unjust that all of them should be punished because that dumbbell Danilo had passed out on the maneuver.

A short captain got out of the jeep, furious at being sent into the field in weather like this.

"Fucking hell, group leader!" he bawled. "What's this fuck-up all about?"

The captain spat into the dust. The wind carried off the saliva. "Who allowed you to send out the soldiers in weather like this?"

Santillez held his tongue. His face paled, he looked even sicker.

"You'll end up before a military court for this, damn it! According to service regulations, the army must not work during a sandstorm! Did you know that? Did you know?"

"But, captain…"

"No 'buts' about it. Send the men back to camp! Immediately! For your 'but' you'll end up in a military court!"

"Yes, captain," Santillez acquiesced.

"And another thing," the captain went on more calmly, "who's Danilo here?"

"That's me, sir." Danilo came forward.

"Get in the jeep. You're to report to Major Karamark."

Santillez looked at Danilo with irritation. This son of a bitch was saving himself while the rest of them would break their backs in the desert. Outwardly composed, Santillez addressed the captain:

"Captain, the soldier you want has frostbitten fingers. He shouldn't leave the camp as he's receiving medical treatment."

The captain spat.

"Fucking hell! Am I the captain here or a damned nurse?" He was red in the face from annoyance. "Don't give me medical treatment! He's to report to the major at once! Let the major deal with that problem over there! They're sitting there doing nothing in that outpost anyway."

No one dared speak any more. The captain had said it all in a few words.

The jeep set off. Danilo had never looked forward to a drive more in his life. He clenched his fingers into a fist. He no longer felt any pain. He was filled with endless bliss. The sand beating on the front windscreen had a strangely calming effect. Everything gave off an air of solemn calm. Both the driver, neat and deodorized, and the captain, whose thoughts were wandering. Danilo stank from his period spent in the desert. Lost in admiration, he stared at the long, white, well-manicured fingers of the driver. The captain had already forgotten the military court and the sallow-looking group leader.

"Calling Thin Snake," came a call over the radio receiver. "The morning hours have golden mouths."

"Fucking hell!" the captain murmured. "It'll be war!" he said yawning.

He stretched himself, reaching out with both arms up to the windscreen.

Around them as far as the eye could see there was an expanse of stony ground with the occasional thorn bush. The area beyond the barbed wire was thickly planted with tripwire mines. Not a living thing that crawled or walked could violate the border of the Roman Empire.

"I repeat," came the cold, impersonal voice, "The morning hours have golden mouths."

The sky was low and gray beneath the gusts of sand.

That night Santillez died in convulsions. The soldiers stood helplessly round his bed, not knowing how to help him. Santillez gave a sudden start and roared in an unknown tongue:

"¡No quiero la vida! ¡No quiero la vida!..."

Then he suddenly went quiet. His wide-open eyes were staring somewhere in the distance. His lips moved weakly in an attempt to say something. As if bewitched, he smiled, and so he died, smiling.

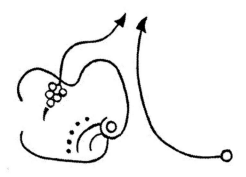

17
Secret Message

"Do you know why I called you here?" the major shouted at Danilo.
"Yes, I know, sir! I passed out during the attack."
"Like hell you know anything!"
"Yes, sir!"
"Do you have any wish in life?"
"Yes, sir. Since I was a lad, I've dreamed of becoming a doctor. When I finish my military service, I would like to study medicine."
"Study where?"
"In Rome."
"When you finish your military service!" the major repeated mockingly. "And do you know when that will be? Never! As long as the war's on, military service won't end. And we always have a war going on! The empire is defended out here in the desert, not in Rome!"
"Yes, sir."
"Do you realize that I can make your dream come true?"
Danilo looked at him in surprise.
"Why did I call you here?" asked the major. "To make your dream come true?"
"I don't know, sir!"
"Do you see? Eh?" — the major gave a triumphant grin. "Didn't I tell you don't know a thing?"
His eyebrows suddenly furrowed. His face darkened menacingly. From his pocket he withdrew the sealed letter and handed it to Danilo.
"You are to take a secret message to Lutetia."
"But that's at the other end of the empire?" Danilo said in amazement as he took the letter.
"That's why it's an important assignment. Listen to me! Tomorrow you'll be given a horse. You will deliver the message to the New Future

prison. Afterwards, you'll leave the horse at the nearest military post. Here's the address" — he showed Danilo a piece of paper. "Have you memorized it?"

"Yes, sir."

"Are you sure?"

"I'm sure!" Danilo confirmed. "When do I get my travel order?"

The major returned the piece of paper to his pocket. He picked up a form already signed from his desk.

"Take it! This order will cover you if you're stopped by the military police. Don't get into an argument with them. If things get hot, no one will help you. Do you understand? Don't make me say it again! First, you take the message to New Future. Then, hand in the horse where I told you. To the duty officer, in person! Then, when they stamp your order, you're free! That stamp means release from the army. Take off your uniform and go wherever you like. You can go to Rome. Study, do whatever you like. Back here you'll be declared unfit. Here, take it!"

"Yes, sir!"

"What's that?" — he caught Danilo by the palms of his hands.

"It's the cold," the young man muttered, shrinking from the major's clammy touch.

"Sugar in the blood? It seems you're a sitting target for just about every disease there is. That's why you want to become a doctor! To cure yourself!"

Danilo made no reply. The major dismissed him with an ill-tempered gesture.

"Now get moving! At once!"

"Yes, sir!"

"And don't forget! You'd better lose your life rather than lose that message! If your horse comes to grief, use your brains and find some other way!"

18
Journey To Rome

THE ROMAN ARMY used only geldings for riding since they were faster and had greater staying power. Their horses were thin. People innocently suppose that all horses graze freely in fields, chewing the cud. Roman horses got nosebags tied behind their ears and filled with a mixture of barley and hay. They were fed exclusively at night. They were groomed only at sunrise. At that time they were bridled and they were not given any water before noon.

Danilo set out on a horse like this for Lutetia. He rode at a gallop as far as the sea. Then he followed the coast to the first port. He embarked on a cargo ship. At first, the ship's master did not want to take him on board. He disagreed with having an animal on his ship! He tried to persuade the soldier to find some other vessel. But the sailors protested. The army aroused great awe in most Romans. And every member of the crew was aware that it was harder to be a soldier than a sailor. So the commander changed his mind. He hurried to fill out the time chart and bill of lading. He did not have the stomach to argue, for this would only have led to unnecessary delay. And he did not wish to lose his bonus for saved time on account of a miserable soldier.

Danilo sat on the wooden floor of the upper deck. He traveled over the great sea. All his past life vanished like a bad dream. The hate-filled Santillez, the desert, and the grass locusts. An unexpected decision by a headstrong captain had resulted in Danilo being transported to a new world, far from Santillez. One word from the major was enough to change the course of Danilo's life and to lift him out of the desert and set him down in Rome. A single word from a complete stranger was stronger than all Danilo's own efforts so far.

Drunk with happiness, Danilo sat back on his scant luggage. The rocking of the boat and the heat of the sun made him drowsy. He looked contentedly at the rough sea and the distant headland. He was growing increasingly tired. His heavy eyelids slowly closed. He heard the splashing of the waves as the scent of the sea and the scent of the wind carried him off into the land of sleep.

He saw a beautiful woman, with a wonderful figure and long red hair. She was standing on a steep inaccessible cliff, wearing a long white silk dress. Her gaze was resolute, but kind. A destructive storm tide crashed with its full force against the sharp reefs. The roar of the sea drowned out the screaming of the winds beating against the rock. This gorgeous vision rose above the deafening noise of the watery abyss. The sea winds tore at the edges of her gown. But her red hair remained unruffled, dark against a pale cloudless and windless sky.

A gentle smile played on her silent lips. Losing all sense of space, Danilo had the impression that the woman was standing in front of him. Entranced by her bewitching beauty, he wanted to touch her cheek with his fingertips. At that moment the coast was lost to view. The lovely redhead was unattainable.

The tide was rising and the waters were roaring, diving into dark eddying whirlpools. Her enchanting smile seemed to be mixed with a sadness at not being able to approach him. An unbridled wave crashed against the jagged cliffs. It threw out three fishes onto the hollow rock. When the water receded, the three fishes in the sea foam turned into three snakes. When Danilo looked again towards the cliff, the woman was no longer there. Only three snakes, their forked tongues darting, were slithering towards that lonely spot.

19
White Powder

IN THE DEEP of night running steps echoed along the corridors of the prison administration. A loud argument was audible. Someone swore. Lights came on. Again, threats were heard. Abaddon got up from his bed and quickly donned his uniform. There was the sound of knocking at the door.

"Come in!" Abaddon shouted in a foul temper. He rubbed his eyes, trying to wake up.

Into the room walked the head of the reform service. He was out of breath. In one hand he was holding a piece of paper, while he held onto the table with the other. He barely got the words out:

"Warden, we're in trouble!"

Abaddon looked at him sleepily. Frowning, he looked at his orderly who was holding out the paper.

"A soldier has brought a message from State Security!"

"So what if it's from State Security?" he said, ignoring the paper.

"That Rinaldo is a Roman citizen!"

A dark shadow flashed across the warden's face. In a second he was completely awake. "Impossible! That's impossible!"

"Warden, everyone thought it was impossible."

"But my citizenship has cost me half my life."

"He was born a Roman citizen, warden."

Enraged, his hands clenched behind his back, he bowed his head for a second and was silent. All of a sudden, he roared:

"You fucking thieves! Drunkards! Lechers! Now I'm the one that has to sort out your pile of shit!"

The head of the reform service stood rooted to the spot, terrified. After his headlong rush, he was barely able to control his heavy breathing. He had to stand absolutely still. And it was this calm that he tried to soothe Abaddon.

"What is it? What are you waiting for?" howled the warden. His bloodshot eyes opened wide. "What are you waiting for, you fucking thief? Get the man out! Get the man out if you don't want to end up in his place!"

It was only when this man had run off that Abaddon took the letter where, on the purple imperial seal, it was written **LORD, YOURS IS THE HEAVEN AND MINE THE EARTH**, and the certificate which had been verified twice once by the Ministry of Education and once by the Ministry of the Interior.

"There's something very wrong here," he grumbled to himself. "I knew from the first day. He looked like trouble. Bad luck follows him! They'll send investigators from Rome."

The frantic blowing of whistles could be heard all over the prison. Accompanied by blows and shouts from the warders, the sleepy prisoners ran out to line up. The siren screamed. They were convinced that Rinaldo was about to get his just desserts. After the roll was called, they were stripped naked and a stinking white powder poured over them. It was getting light. The day began with fear. They shaved all the prisoners' heads and started searching for lice.

"It's the plague!" the whisper spread.

Petrified, the prisoners fell silent. For the first sign of the plague is madness. They scrubbed the tables in the dining-hall with sand all day long. Then the wooden floors in the dormitories. They whitewashed the walls and, for the first time, took out the bed-linen to be aired. No one ever saw again the wretch who walked on all fours. The confused warders told the prisoners that Rinaldo had been released. And not only that he had walked free, but that he had also insisted that Abaddon come to his cell in solitary and apologize to him. The prisoners were even more scared by these stories. The whole world seemed to have gone crazy. True, Rinaldo did not appear. And if they had already found him dead, why did they need to put on that performance with the powder? Unless they wanted to calm people down with lies and make it easier to kill them later.

That night Rinaldo avoided a cruel punishment. The other prisoners had not forgiven him for talking to the old man accused of raping his own daughter. The screws on the legs of Rinaldo's bed had been loosened that night. The coverlet had already been soaked in heating oil. If he had not been suddenly set free, Rinaldo, trapped between the chain and the collapsed bed, would have been burned alive.

From the window of his room, Abaddon supervised the hurried cleaning operation in silence. "I hope they finish up before the investigators arrive!" he thought nervously.

In the end, the rumor ran among the prisoners that Rinaldo had been contagious and that was the reason why he had been liquidated by the prison guards themselves.

20
Kristina, My Beloved

AS SOON AS he arrived in Lutetia, Rinaldo made for Kristina's apartment.

On the door was a plate with an unknown name. Rinaldo pressed the bell. The door was opened by a short ugly man. He stared at the excited young man in amazement. He had never heard of Kristina. He did not know who had occupied the apartment before him.

Rinaldo went down to the janitor on the ground floor. The unpleasant man was angry that the unannounced visitor had interrupted him in the middle of his meal.

"I remember you!" said the janitor, wiping his mouth with his hand.

Rinaldo was overjoyed hoping that this meant the end of his search.

"I remember you! You used to come and visit that young girl upstairs. Who knows where she is now. She went off somewhere. Don't ask me, typical female!"

He banged the door in the young man's face.

As he went out into the street, Rinaldo turned to look once again at the familiar building. The plaster was falling off the large façade and you could see darkened brick underneath. Rinaldo realized only now just how truly ugly the whole building was. He had not noticed the broken windows pasted over with newspaper before. Kristina has transmitted her beauty and cheerfulness to the half-dead world around her. Because of her he had once loved this building.

Stifling warm winds were blowing.

Now he recalled with sadness her smile and long blonde hair. He remembered the skin on the fingers and palms of her hands grown rough from boiling up artist's colors. His friend Kristina now seemed to him to have been both his sister and his lover.

He ran to the Academy.

"Yes, yes! Kristina was our best student. I recall her painting of the horseman," said her old professor, as he looked absently into the distance.

"But where is she now?"

"I don't know," continued the professor in an even tone. "Even today when I think of that painting, I think of it as showing a hero afraid. On a white horse, charging, with his sword drawn. The maddened horse champed on the bit. You could see fear in the eyes of the warrior. He was afraid, but he attacked the enemy nonetheless. It was a very successful portrayal of contradictions. Only someone like Kristina could have done it! Love! Even a picture like that exuded love. Almost all artists seem to move us by evoking unpleasant feelings. The world is short of beauty, of tenderness, of love."

"Please sir, I've been looking everywhere for Kristina," Rinaldo cut in.

The professor raised his eyebrows angrily.

"Now just you listen! I think there's been enough vulgarity. And why am I even bothering to talk about art to you!"

Turning his back, he left without another word. Rinaldo went after him. He thought of apologizing. But then he realized that this would be pointless. He walked out of the school.

Outside the winds continued the blow and the sun was shining.

Rinaldo went through the telephone directory. Her name was nowhere. Yesterday he could not even imagine leaving prison. Now he was free, but without Kristina. He yearned for her smile. She would hold his hand, skipping down the stairs, telling him of some king from Tula who never took a drink.

"Kristina, where are you now?" he cried in despair.

He had never been able to tell her of his sudden arrest. Perhaps she believed he had abandoned her.

She had once painted a horseman, strong, charging with his steed. In his bright uniform and armed to the teeth, he looked frightening. But the horseman was tied to his saddle. Rinaldo had laughed:

"What kind of a horseman are these, Kristina, that are tied to their saddles?"

"This hero has a broken leg, Rinaldo. He had an accident when a young officer. Since then he has been frightened of duels. But he is a hero and so he charges."

"Why does the poor unfortunate go on fighting?"

"It is you and I who are unfortunate, Rinaldo. That man fights because he wants to go to heaven. Will the two of us go to heaven? Do we have too many sins to be forgiven?"

Rinaldo, crestfallen, held his peace.

"All right! Kristina smiled and kissed him on the neck. "We won't talk about sins. Can you jump three stairs at a time, podgy Rinaldo?"

She pinched him gently on the stomach. "Or perhaps you're better at knowing how to say 'stair' in Aramaic? Stair? So, how do you say 'stair' in Aramaic?"

She would put her arms round him. They would walk slowly and she would rest her head on his shoulder.

"Rinaldo, it would be wonderful if we could live in the south. The corns ripening at this time. And it's warm."

Rinaldo started to weep.

"Kristina, I've done it!"

"Kristina, they've accepted me in Rome!"

Rinaldo was not being honest with himself. There was no horseman in the painting. Or rather, there was no clearly recognizable shape in the painting. The vivid brush strokes of yellow, red and blue merged into one another revealing Kristina's restless temperament. Rinaldo's love stifled Kristina and she had left him before he was arrested. There was nobody to mourn for Rinaldo when he was in prison.

21
Confession

You who bring me dreams
Sadness
Youth
A forgotten world,
Life is longing for you
But
That is you
A tender drifting scent
A gentle smile
A silken touch
And the trembling of your body when fear vanishes
As you snuggle up to me
The pain lies in remembrance
Restlessness
Fearing and waiting

22
A Gnashing Of Teeth

DANILO AND RINALDO arrived in Rome by same train from Lutetia, neither knowing the other existed. In the mass of newly arrived passengers, the two of them, each with their own worries, set off in different directions. At the first step, they were both amazed by the street musicians and dancers.

Masked, covered with colored feathers, with drums beating, the dancers swayed to and fro and stepped forward and back. Their bare bodies painted in bright colors, glistened in the sun. They waved bundles of dried grass. Their leader blew some inflammable liquid at a flaming hoop, the handle of which he gripped in his outstretched right hand. Inside the hoop a beaten metal snake burned. Only the nearest bystanders could discern that the snake had two legs and that, like a man, it stood erect on two legs. This peculiar device spread smoke across the pavement, reaching up to the dancers' knees. The rustling leaves and the roar of the fire accompanied the singers and the beating drums.

Spellbound, Rinaldo and Danilo moved nearer to the dancers.

"It's the leaves of the wind rustling," Rinaldo recalled, quite forgetting that he was in a strange city.

Lost in admiration, he remembered the men who had healed him long ago.

The first thing Danilo noticed was the smoke. The awareness of choking and of fire attracted him. He shuddered, thinking of the military exercise. On that occasion he had almost been asphyxiated by the smoke. Horrified, he still could not believe that he was free.

The passers-by usually did not hang around very long. On one side, a street sweeper, leaning on his birch broom, his eyes full of scorn, awaited for the performance to end. He knew from experience that these street idlers always left the greatest mess. He did not dream that the movements of the dancers' arms were summoning up invisible forces.

Danilo and Rinaldo stood facing each other, separated by the dancers. Through the fire Danilo remembered a hooked nose and a resolute gaze. The face of the unknown youth was drawn and gaunt with suffering. But his dark eyes radiated a deep strength. From the other side, Rinaldo noticed a gentle face that had also known much trouble.

This chance meeting of eyes was to change the course of their lives.

Danilo turned on his heel and left. He was frightened by the resolve in the stranger's eyes. As he moved away from the crowd, he could not rid himself of the shame he felt at his own weakness. But he forgot everything when he lifted his eyes and beheld the beauty of the clear blue sky. Instead of the deafening music of the street players, complete silence reigned. The square was encircled by white marble pillars. High up on each pillar stood the statue of a ruler or a general. Pigeons alighted on the stone crowns and brandished swords. These victors of ancient wars, clothed in stone cloaks and armor and covered in bird droppings, surveyed their former territories. The stone rulers stood in the middle of their empire, whose forgotten distant frontiers were still marked by forgotten marble boundary stones. The stone generals watched over remote military cemeteries in the desert with headstone memorials cracked from the sun. At the foot of the monuments were scarcely legible inscriptions which the wind had eroded:

> *Here lies the fame of Rome,*
> *A bigger or more renowned city the sun has never seen.*

When he woke up from his daydream, Danilo understood that he was in a strange city. He was alone in Rome, forced to fight for survival. He was dirty and hungry. He only had enough money to buy a newspaper for the adverts and a plan of the city. He did not fear uncertainty. He had been penniless even before he joined the army. And he was comforted by the thought that, after his persecution at the hands of Santillez, any new problems would be child's play.

He breathed a sigh of relief when he came upon an advert for a job as a stable boy. They only gave the address, no telephone number. He got upset when he looked at the city plan that the estate indicated by the address was a long way out.

But he had no choice.

There was no path back from Rome. In any case, he had nowhere to go back to. He hurried, for he had to find something before dark. You don't discuss a job at night.

Danilo set off on foot towards the out-of-town estate. Along the way he looked at Rome, luxurious and splendid. This was a gilded Rome, with shining fountains, well-trimmed soft lawns, and white stone houses. Danilo did not have the money for this Rome. Yet great wealth was linked to great poverty. The life of most of Rome's citizens was not as splendid as the people who lived overseas in distant provinces imagined. The road soon led Danilo through a part of the city with rotting wooden shacks and ruins with tin roofs. The people who dwelt in these dens looked tired, faded and indifferent. They were dirty, had a red unhealthy complexion, sickly eyes, and were vomit-stained and crippled. It was as if they expected that the world's city of light would conquer this loss of hope. This degree of poverty could be seen nowhere except in the world's most beautiful city.

The day was ending. To pay for an overnight in Rome, you needed two weeks' hard labour in some provincial field. The job offer of stable boy was the sole opportunity to find some form of shelter.

The gate was opened by an elderly man, probably the estate janitor. He poked his head through and gave Danilo a distrustful look. He was silent.

"I read your advertisement!" said Danilo.

"Tell me lad, have you worked with horses?" he asked coolly, without a greeting.

"Yes, I have, sir," Danilo concurred.

The old man shook his head suspiciously. Danilo didn't look like a hale and hearty stable boy.

"And just where did you work with horses?"

"In the army, sir."

The janitor threw the door wide open. They set off towards the stables.

"Yes, you're right. You can learn anything there. It's the army! I served, too, in the eastern desert. Ugh, that was a time, I can tell you! Not like today. Today you can do anything. But before, ugh! No, that's the truth, not when an order came through…"

The janitor loosened his tongue. Danilo was happy, and visibly relieved, as he listened to that divine chattering. The old man was in a good mood now. At least for the moment, Danilo had wrenched himself out of the world of the deprived. That was a world of weeping and gnashing of teeth.

23
Mark On The Forehead

RINALDO DID NOT KNOW why his eyes followed the young man disappearing into the distance. He sensed that some misfortune was troubling the young man and that he was lonely. In his sad eyes and lack of confidence he seemed to recognize an element of his own fate. He averted his gaze.

One of the dancers was moving bound in chains. Powerless because of his hands chained behind his back, he could hardly breathe. All of a sudden, to the admiration of all present, he freed himself from his fetters with a single tug. Arms outstretched in pride, he tossed the chains aside.

Thinking of the prison, Rinaldo turned away. He walked with slow steps. The vision of the tossed chains reminded him that he was free. He raised his head and unconsciously looked up at the stone rulers and stone generals. Many of them were had had their noses and ears knocked off.

"The first thing to rot on dead men are their noses and ears," thought Danilo.

Then he noticed that the sun was shining out of a clear sky and that it was a fine day. He could no longer see the sad-eyed youth. The street players continued to repeat their monotonous movements as they passed through the smoke.

On leaving prison, he had unexpectedly been given a lot of money on which he could survive the next few months. He was hungry and went to buy something to eat.

The food seller, a fat, over-decorated chatterbox, could hardly wait to strike up a conversation with someone. Noticing that Rinaldo was a foreigner, she was very happy. Her eyes, round which she had slapped thick layers of dark green eye-shadow, grew wide with excitement.

"Yes, sir, we all came to Rome from God knows where. I came from the north, sixteen years ago. Rome changes everyone. You get used to it. My daughters have just come back from visiting relatives in the old country. It's terrible down there! They don't want to go back there ever again. How can two young ladies, brought up in Rome, go down there among those primitive people? They're a lazy people, rude and bad-mannered. Good manners, sir, are the sign of an educated man. They distinguish us from the animals. The blasphemers are wrong when they say man is descended from monkeys. No, sir! You can't take a monkey and educate it to be noble and cultivated. No, our blessed emperor has allowed all sorts of freedom, and as a result people now say what they like. It's well-known how you handle degenerates. Our emperor offers everyone a chance. People arrive here, they look like scarecrows. No one at all knows where they come from. Yet Emperor Bonifacio feeds them all and lets them live. I was barefoot when I came to Rome. And just look what I have now!"

She spread out her arms proudly towards the shelves with sacks of flour. Tireless, she continued her story:

"If it wasn't for me, sir, this entire suburb would be left without food. And if someone happens to ask you, young man, to tell them about Rome, watch your step!" — the voice dropped to a whisper, as she turned cautiously towards the empty shop. "The world is full of informers. Always speak well of Rome and of your own land. It's disgusting to hear people from the provinces saying how much they admire Rome and how they scorn their own country. Don't ever forget that. True, there's nothing here that a man would complain of. The only thing that isn't settled is citizenship. It can't be got at any price! But, you're young, sir. Do your damnedest! I guess in time the laws will change."

"I already have citizenship!" Rinaldo interrupted.

The woman was struck dumb. She stared at him in admiring awe. Without uttering another word, she handed him his provisions.

Leaving the shop, Rinaldo walked away slowly. He felt he was losing his strength. Suddenly he stumbled. With his last ounce of energy, he grabbed hold of a lamppost. He was shivering as if stricken with fever. He wept, his forehead pressed against the post. The weeping became more painful. His lower jaw was trembling. The inquisitive food-seller came out into the street and stared at him. As he pushed himself away from the lamppost, Rinaldo tottered and fell.

"The man's going to die!" screamed the woman, running out to the unconscious Rinaldo.

Terrified, she did not know what to do. Rinaldo was lying on his back, stiff as a corpse. His head remained in the air, as if he was floating, laid out on an invisible pillow.

"The man's going to die!" the woman wailed. "The Roman's going to die!"

She surreptitiously kept one eye fixed on the entrance to the shop. Rinaldo lay completely rigid, holding his head in a ghostly pose. In the distance, on the opposite side of the street, the dancers were repeating their monotonous movements in the smoke as if in a trance.

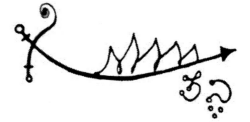

24
A Nervous Horse

AT THE ESTATE, Danilo started into work he had never done before. Besides him, several other boys were employed on the estate. He learned fast by looking at what they did. However, Danilo used his first free pass into the city to submit an application for enrolment in Medical School.

After only a few weeks, something totally unexpected occurred on the estate. That day, Danilo had been assigned the task of feeding the youngest foal. He knew that the animal was nervous. At one moment he was stroking the foal. The animal started to flinch at his touch. Danilo tenderly put his arms round it. He whispered to it, trying to soothe the animal, convinced that this weak creature was simply scared of an unknown stable boy. But as he went to put his arms round the animal's neck, the foal fell down onto its forelegs. Then it collapsed on the floor. Its whole body was shaking. It neighed in pain as if its stomach had been pierced by an arrow. Tossing its head, already in its death throes, the foal vomited through its nostrils.

Danilo closed his eyes. Human voices could be heard in the general alarm. Never in his life had Danilo seen a horse throwing up. He had never believed that he could harm anyone.

"See what you've done?" the head groom roared at Danilo. "Do you have any idea how much a pedigree foal costs?"

"But he didn't do anything!" rejoined the janitor.

"From the very first day I felt he would bring us nothing but trouble!" the head groom grumbled.

As evening approached, the mare got upset when she didn't see her foal. It was useless trying to calm her. They put another blanket under her, but nothing helped.

"There's nothing to be done for it," the old janitor said in a very quiet tone. "An animal's like a human being."

Danilo didn't know what to say.

"The same as a human being," continued the old man, "even more so. A horse can sense a flood and death. What can a man sense? Nothing! Absolutely nothing!"

The mare could not be comforted. Danilo was the new boy and the other animals feared him even more. That evening the stable was filled with unrest. Danilo tried to be gentle. He spoke in child's language to the horses and brushed them carefully. But nothing was any good. Fear entered the animals whenever Danilo came near them. Whinnying distractedly, the horses reared out of control to avoid his touch.

"Go to bed!" the old janitor ordered Danilo and handed him a letter. "The postman brought this today. Sorry, I forgot to give to you earlier. This incident completely threw me. It's not your fault! The head groom envies you because he knows full well this isn't the place for you. And animals are even more sensitive than people."

Danilo left in silence. The well-meant words of comfort bothered him, that this wasn't the place for him. He suspected that the envelope contained a written dismissal. Concerned for the future, he went to his room. He didn't open the letter until he had had a bath and got ready for bed. The letterhead took his breath away. It was the Medical School.

Dear Sir,

This is to confirm receipt of your application to enroll at the Medical School and we wish to thank you for your interest.

You will be informed of the result of your application in due course. As an applicant, permanently domiciled outside Rome, you are entitled to assistance in finding temporary work. If need be, we would kindly ask you to contact Mr Antoine, the owner of the Night Wind club.

From the Student Service

25
A Clock That Doesn't Tell The Time

or The Tale of a Search for Happiness

FOR A LONG TIME Doctor Natasha Shapiro stared through the window at the sundial in the hospital grounds. She thought of her son. Since her divorce, she had conducted an unsuccessful search for someone to look after and teach her seven-year-old son Ari while she was at work. Her transfer to the Student Service had completely upset her. She was devastated by the youth of the students with whom she came in contact.

It was cloudy. The tip of a pointed iron bar round which was curled a wrought iron snake rose from among the numbers where it had been impaled. The iron bar threw no shadow. The sundial didn't tell the time. For the umpteenth time she read the inscription under the trailing tail of the snake:

The days are like a passing shadow
And I am like dried grass.

She recalled her first student days in the city of Padua. How she marched excitedly down the corridors of the Faculty. She gazed with awe at the walls covered with photographs of students from earlier generations. She deceived herself into thinking that she was high-spirited and cheerful, as if nothing had changed for years within her being. The freshmen in Rome looked too young, like children. Their youth confirmed to her that she was no longer young.

Natasha Shapiro stood with an absent look. Her sadness was betrayed only by the lack of luster in her long blonde hair.

"Dr Shapiro, you seem to be in luck!" the head nurse addressed her. "It looks as if we've found a tutor for young Ari."

Natasha Shapiro was shocked. She appeared to have wakened out of a dream. In the same moment, she forgot about the irretrievable lost time.

"We're about to let one of our future students go. He fainted in the street last night."

"It's not epilepsy?"

"No, absolutely not! That's what we thought at first. It was just fatigue, exhaustion! He's only just arrived in Rome."

The nurse managed to capture Natasha's attention.

"This one speaks all languages! We didn't know he was a Roman, so we put him in the foreigners' ward. He spoke to every single patient in his own language."

Natasha had not expected that the Student Service would find someone to tutor her son. Even for menial jobs like this it was necessary that students possess Roman citizenship. She hoped that this budding student would accept the offer of a room and pocket money. Something told her that this person had been searching for a long time.

With hurried steps, Natasha and the head nurse arrived at the reception desk. Rinaldo was waiting for his release form to be certified. Visible on the left side of his face was a scratch that began on the cheekbone, vanished near the eye, and ended up on his forehead.

"He sometimes scratches himself in his sleep!" whispered the head nurse with a smile.

Standing before him Rinaldo saw a beautiful woman in her late thirties. Her beauty, no longer youthful, had come to full maturity at an age when her contemporaries in Catalonia had already lost their bloom. Natasha Shapiro liked Rinaldo's calm, resolute expression.

The nurses, who had lifted the unconscious Rinaldo onto a stretcher the day before, were clumsily filling in the record. If Mrs Shapiro had known that Rinaldo slept with his head raised, she would never have taken him into her house. That first indication of serious mental illness went unnoticed.

26
When The Sun Was God

THE CEREMONY TO FOUND THE UNIVERSITY had been planned for the early evening. Torches were burning round the main square. The façade of the imperial palace was separated from the crowd by wall of fire. People were pushing forward, gazing in admiration at the spacious inset balcony from where the emperor addressed them on important occasions. And Bonifacio, the emperor of all emperors, the father of fathers, the supreme commander of the armed forces of heaven and earth, the lord of the great city of Rome, the ruler of both Bosphoruses (in Turkey and the Crimea), Libya, Catalonia, Galatia, Cappadoccia, Thrace, Colchida, Cilicia, Morocco, Ethiopia, and countless provinces, cold and warm seas and the southern islands, was with his people this time, too. But the emperor did not approach the rostrum during the ceremony. He stood back, surrounded by his leading administrators. Only the Roman dignitaries gathered on the balcony were in a position to notice that the most holy Bonifacio was not in a good mood. He said nothing the whole time. It seemed that lord of the world had come to this significant event after a sleepless night. In any case, it was José who was supposed to give the speech, as Minister of Education.

To an onlooker the not too bright and definitely malicious Vicena was standing apart. He stared at the ruler for a long time. He was not at all pleased by the emperor's indifference. The entire empire feared Vicena. It was said that that he even tapped Bonifacio's phone. With his secret police he spread terror everywhere and thus controlled the lives and dreams of the Empire's subjects. He was a man of few words. If he did take part in a conversation, his face would take on a vacant look, and anyone who did not know him would soon be persuaded that the minister was hopelessly stupid. Now, as the Roman dignitaries nudged each other, joking about the emperor's drowsiness, only Vicena had the impression that Bonifacio was sick.

José bowed to Vicena. But in line with the requirements of the service, for time had helped him grow accustomed to maintaining outwardly friendly relations even with people he did not like. Before he started to speak, he threw another glance at the lord of the police. For the umpteenth time he saw the usual, deceptively bovine expression. As was his wont, Vicena's eyes were wandering in a vacant fashion as if he was thinking of something else and not paying attention.

A soldier in a white uniform stepped smartly out in front of José. With a flaming silver baton he set alight the two torches located to the right and left of the minister. To a roar of applause from the assembled crowd, José began his speech:

"You have come from all corners of the empire. You are living witnesses to the founding of the University. I must admit that we thought long and hard about taking this decision. You yourselves know that the universities of Bologna and Padua started teaching a long time ago, and that we hesitated for a number of years. It was too great a responsibility for us. It's a hard thing to admit, but no human wisdom had been well applied until now. Despite that, we are almost in love with ourselves over our new achievements. Now we really have a reason to ridicule our forbears who did not possess that wisdom and, thousands of years ago, wrote the following words:"

He prepared to read out an extract. Bonifacio gave a discreet yawn. He hated old writings. Vicena alone was listening attentively. José resolutely continued:

"This is what those uneducated men wrote:

> "Four sounds of death echoed round the world. When the fifth trumpet call resounded, I saw a star fall from the sky to earth. And a bottomless well opened up, and smoke came from the well like the smoke of a great furnace, and the sky turned black. Locusts came down to earth out of the smoke. And they were told not to damage the grass of the earth nor any green thing, nor any tree, only people. "

José lifted his eyes. Under the light of the flames, his face gleamed in the night.

"You yourselves are aware how uneducated our forefathers were. It's not locusts that will destroy us, ladies and gentlemen, but atomic energy and infectious diseases, the like of which did not exist before. Mankind is now capable of destroying itself in many different ways."

Squeezed by the crowd, Rinaldo gazed at the minister admiringly. At one moment he thought he saw the bulging eyes and rotten teeth of the old man he had met in the prison instead of José's fine features.

"I am the chosen one!" rang in his ears. "I have been chosen to save the world!"

"Still, our age is very different from the age of ancient states where wisdom and knowledge were only available to a very narrow circle of people. Today we laugh at that. Yet I have to say that that narrow circle of people was responsible both for its own works and for the people to whom they were to reveal their knowledge. I do not know any example like what is happening here today. When knowledge became accessible to all men, evil came to rule the world. We are not able to tame that genie and return it to the magic lamp."

Vicena's face again took on its vacant expression.

"We did not achieve anything good in preventing the founding of our University. All we got was the accusation that we were blocking progress and that the time in which we live is already being called the dark ages. Not even the decision to set up a medical school instead of a technical school was of any help. Although medicine today is still benevolent, a time will come when people will be able to change the shape of the living world — animals, plants, even themselves. At first, that will bring a lot of benefits, bigger animals and bigger harvests. But no one will be responsible for that knowledge. And it will be available to everyone. Sad at the wrong turning the human race has taken, I have been given the task of opening the University. Future generations will celebrate this day, unaware of what is to come. However, on reflection, this is a great moment as it leads towards that day of reckoning. Then our planet, cleansed of impurity, will become green again and the whole universe will be at peace. The world will become lovelier. Among all the inventions of human wisdom, you will be able to look down from the heavenly heights and see a huge, ridiculous wall in Asia. That work will speak of its creators. But there will be no creators anywhere. Your task, as students, is to use your scientific achievements to make sure that inexorable day dawns as soon as possible. The more famous you become, the more celebrated will be our University. And with it, His Majesty, our holy and eternal Emperor of the Galatians."

There was an eruption of cheers. Accompanied by clapping and shouting, José drew back. Bonifacio stepped forward in his place.

Everyone was glad the University was now founded, that the human race was no longer on the wrong path. In the great clamor that had started before he finished his speech, no one even noticed that José was promising fame to the immortal Emperor of the Galatians, and not to Bonifacio, Emperor of the Romans. In that moment of celebration, no one considered it important as Galatia had long since been brought to heel. Under the laws of Rome, the Roman emperor was at the same time Emperor of the Galatians. Even mentioning the immortal emperor stirred no one. As a mark of great respect, Bonifacio was treated to as an immortal being.

Vicena gazed upon the excited students with contempt. He knew that this rabble had come to Rome to get citizenship and employment at court, not to fight for the day to dawn when people would live on a greener earth. When there would be no more wars, no more army. And if there were no army, there would be no more police. But there had to be some kind of police in that new future when people had everything they needed. Yes, the army wasn't exactly a must. But the police was different. Wherever there were people, there had to be order.

The emperor blessed the University.

A vibrant beating of drums exploded. Illuminated rockets swished up in the air. Cutting through the night, they burst into countless colored shining dots. As they fell, the dazzling light rekindled, spurting a fiery rain across the whole sky. Nobody appeared to notice the real stars, with their monotonous weak glow. All the wondrous variations of the pyrotechnic art were on display. Flaming mushrooms, winged horses, and a fiery imperial crest. There was joy on earth and in heaven.

The Romans got their University.

Cannon roared in the distance. These were celebratory salvos. Blue flags bearing the cross and eagle unfurled. Flushed street musicians beat their drums. Wine flowed and food was given out. The singing of drunken citizens was heard. Complete strangers embraced each other in the streets. The imperial cavalry, lined up in their red ceremonial uniforms, lent weight to the scene through their dignified bearing.

Rome's dignitaries withdrew inside the palace to celebrate. Even the emperor's spirits improved that evening. His tired face that had seemed to be hiding some sort of pain became bright again. Holding a crystal goblet in his left hand, he patted Vicena on the shoulder with the right. But the glass fell from his hand and shattered on the floor. Red wine spread over the mat, over the woven golden sun.

"That's a good sign!" those nearest shouted in unison. "When a glass breaks, that's a good sign!"

The servants rushed to pick up the pieces.

"He's sick!" Vicena bit his lip. "I knew it! He's sick!"

"May luck be with you, Your Majesty!" those present shouted cheerfully. "It's a good sign!"

Bonifacio joined in the merrymaking, joking about the broken glass. Vicena was sure that evening that the emperor would never pick up anything again.

Everyone was in a glow thinking of the prophesied future. Life was hard at the moment. The Garden of Eden was still to be found beside the river Euphrates. A wall had been put up around it so it was hard to get to. You just had to be patient and wait for the minister's words to come true. Everything he said came true. So it would be with a happier future. Everyone would be brothers then. The wall round the Garden of Eden would become pointless, as the whole earth would be a garden. Of course, there would have to be a wall in Asia as the Euphrates was in Asia.

After he had left the formal rooms, the skinny Minister of Education stood alone on the balcony. For a long time he looked up into the dark vault of the sky, lost in thought. At first, he had viewed the general carousing with contempt. The absurd explosions of the fireworks served only to illustrate the superficiality and stupidity of the human race. But then he recalled that in Galatia, too, people had announced the birth of a child or some other happy event by firing into the air. Someone had celebrated thus when he was born. He was sad that night and deaf to the laughter and music that could be heard at every step.

There was a smell of burning in the air. The pale night stars once again emerged in the clear sky. The merrymaking did not flag. The drums continued throbbing and there came the sound of rattles. Rome's citizens looked forward to the day when the earth would be cleansed of dirt and grime. Because then the world would be more beautiful.

27
The Best Place In Rome

"RINALDO, WE HAVE TO CELEBRATE THIS," Mrs Shapiro laughed. In her hands she held an opened letter.

The young man looked perplexed.

"I asked the Student Service to find me a tutor for Ari!" she explained. "Today they recommended you to me! Isn't that wonderful? It seems it was fated for us to meet before this letter from the Student Service. We have succeeded in beating fate to it!"

Rinaldo could not help laughing himself.

"So it was a good choice!" Natasha Shapiro went on in a happy voice. "And a good choice must be celebrated! Tonight I'm taking you to the best place in Rome."

28
A Mistake Corrected

NOT KNOWING OF THE OTHER'S EXISTENCE, Rinaldo and Danilo sent in applications for enrolment in the Medical School. The two young men certified their documents on previous education with the same notary.

The police clerk in the Student Service whose job it was to copy down details of the applicants stopped dead in his tracks. At first he thought that the same details had been entered under two different numbers. It was only after he had checked them again that he concluded that both these young men who had given in applications without verification from their schools had traveled to Rome the same day from Lutetia. He underlined the two suspicious names in red pencil and added double question marks in the margin. At the end of working hours he handed in the report to his superior.

The police sergeant who received the report was visibly annoyed. On his left cheek he had a scar as if it had been pierced with a knife. As he read the report, the scar started to tremble. He immediately sought information from Lutetia. To his surprise, he learned that that neither Rinaldo nor Danilo were registered in Lutetia on the day they set off for Rome. The sergeant tried to find out where the young men had lived previously. He requested copies of their de-registration forms. He was informed that both young men had only temporarily registered in Rome so they had not needed to have de-registered from their places of permanent residence.

The sergeant feared that he might cause an unnecessary panic through some rash move on his part. So he took an eraser and rubbed out the red question marks. He certified the report on the back with his signature and the stamp: *Read!* He went up to the big wall plan of the city of Rome where his area was marked in yellow. As he checked the details from the report, he stuck two pins outside the yellow area with a sigh of relief.

Danilo and Rinaldo were beyond the sergeant's reach. All the same, he was uneasy and hesitated to hand the suspicious report to the chiefs of the surrounding areas. If he were wrong, he could ruin his reputation and chances of promotion. If he were right, and did nothing about it, his rivals would get all the credit. The order to check students' data fell to him. But he could not tell from the order how important it was. He decided to take matters into his own hands. He would have to move Rinaldo and Danilo to the area for which he was responsible. He took a pair of compasses and measured the distance as if hoping to correct something that life had separated and put outside his reach. He went through the business directory and the address book of informers. He considered the matter long and hard, making sure he did not overlook anything. In a better mood now, he put two new pins inside the yellow area.

That day the foal was poisoned. That same day Danilo was instructed to contact Mr Antoine, owner of the "Night Wind".

That day Mrs Shapiro was given Rinaldo's name by the Student Service.

That day a mistake was corrected.

The sergeant was pleased with a job well done. He could not entertain the possibility of well-organized events taking place without him playing a part in them.

29
The Night Wind

DANILO RECEIVED PRESIDENT ANTOINE, owner of the *Night Wind* club personally. The man liked to be called president, for this lent importance to his club. Overwhelmed by everyday events, rich Romans yearned for something unusual and mysterious. President Antoine knew how to cater to their wishes. He was a well-built man, with a hairy chest and bulging muscles. The top button on his shirt was always left undone. Around his thick neck he wore several heavy gold chains as decoration.

He gazed at Danilo in pity. It was clear to him that Rome did not have a very bright future if it produced such stunted young men. However, he perked up when he noticed from Danilo's accent that he was not from these parts. This time it was not so much because of Rome's future as because rich Romans were extremely fond of a fascinating foreign accent.

"Well, lad, this is how it goes," he began to explain to Danilo, "keep your eyes open!"

The president had assumed a rather stiff stance. As he bowed, he came quite close to Danilo ears. His voice changed and became more decisive, yet at the same time soft and seductive:

"Madam, your eyes are as cold as diamonds. The diamond is the queen of jewels. And there is a jewel in your restless heart, which beats in its loneliness. So why not relax with us tonight. Let us indulge together in passionate beauty."

Changing his voice again, the president addressed Danilo:

"Keep your eyes open, lad! Not everyone tells you everything like me. Style is important. Do as I do, but develop your own style. If you don't, you're finished! You can't get by in Rome like that. But make sure there's an element of imagination! I want everything to be exceptional. To sound like a siren from space. And not some half-baked stupid tricks."

You reached the underground rooms down a winding corridor, illuminated by an unreal green light. The deliberately lowered arch of rough brick was hung with cobwebs in places. By contrast, the polished handrail of lacquered wood and the white marble steps with a soft carpet spoke of a very exclusive venue.

The corridor ended with a black metal door, in front of which stood two doormen in red uniforms. A silver metal eye decorated the door. A silver eyelid would open and beneath the metal eyebrow you could see the pupil of the man looking from the other side. The door would open, and the doormen would bow in greeting. Passing through the door you entered a circular room. The walls were hung with painted scenes from a stony desert, and because of the shape of the room, they seemed unending. The centre of the room was in semi-darkness. You could just make out some low palms whose big leaves shielded tables and comfortable armchairs made of the softest black leather. From the dark central area you could see the unreal scenes, which at midday were bathed in a gentle red glow from the lamps, like at the rising of the desert sun. People moved soundlessly over the soft carpets. There were wafts of lavender and almond-blossom, mingled with the mysterious scent of musk.

A young man with a bony face and soft eyes would approach impressed visitors. Greeting them courteously in a strange accent, he would lead them to vacant seats.

In a niche cut into the underground wall there were armchairs for special guests. On the armchair seats were seated bronze statues, turned in such a way that they were looking at the painted scenes. President Antoine loved spending his time with his dead bronze guests and follow what was happening in the large room, shrouded in the half-dark. He was pleased with Danilo's work. In fact, he was delighted. At the start, the young man had seemed quite inept and there were times when he could not stand him. However, the visitors soon grew to like him. Yet despite everything, Antoine felt that Danilo was unhappy and disappointed. He concluded that the young man did not know what he wanted. Antoine's club was the best-known in Rome. All the jet set came there, the sort of people you did not meet in the street. It was only there that you could meet the most beautiful girls. The *Night Wind* offered everything that a young man coming to Rome could dream of. President Antoine was convinced that Danilo would not become aware of all that was on offer until he lost it.

Danilo quickly got used to his new duties and moved around very freely. But one evening, about ten days after he'd started his new job, they gave him an assistant, who got on his nerves. Whenever Danilo greeted the guests, the assistant would take their coats so clumsily that several times he dropped them. Danilo stepped up the charm to deflect the guests' attention from this lad who was nothing but a hindrance. He barely managed to disguise his annoyance. Memories of the borderlands spurred him on and he was constantly haunted by the fear that if he put just one foot wrong, some evil forces would take him back to that damned wasteland.

That evening, Danilo paid no attention to the police sergeant, disguised as a guest, who watched his every move from an armchair in the dim interior.

At one point in the evening, he started off towards an extraordinarily beautiful blonde woman. She had captivated him at first sight with her figure and dignified bearing. Following her eyes, he went up to her with a gentle smile. Then he found himself rooted to the spot. The blonde woman's escort was none other than the young man he had seen through the smoke immediately upon his arrival in Rome.

From his seat in the dark the police sergeant did not see the surprise on the faces of Danilo and Rinaldo as they met.

The assistant who was standing behind Danilo did not notice any change in Rinaldo's expression. Giving a pre-arranged nod to the sergeant, he confirmed this.

Danilo succeeded in composing himself and showed the visitors to their seats.

Relieved, the sergeant prepared to leave. He had finally convinced himself personally that Danilo and Rinaldo were not acquainted. For since the life path of the two young men had changed, he had issued a surveillance order on them. But in answer to all his questions, he got the reply that the youths were in no way connected. The complicated procedure of establishing mutual acquaintances proved to be unnecessary in their case. Since the death of the foal, Danilo had not talked to anybody anyway. If they had known each other, Rinaldo would certainly have been surprised that Danilo was not at the estate with the horses.

"Do you know that man?" Natasha asked, staring penetratingly into Rinaldo's eyes.

"No! I've never seen him before!"

"Come on; tell me, where do you know him from!" she persisted mysteriously, convinced that he had lied to her.

Rinaldo picked up his drink, without answering.

A little while later the police sergeant made towards the exit. Danilo tried to force a smile, but his face remained too tense and stiff. He tried hard not to look at the visitor's scar on the left cheek. The sergeant struck up the conversation:

"Where're you from, lad?"

"From Thrace."

"You've come a long way to Rome! A person needs a lot of courage to change their life like that!"

"Sometimes even impossible dreams come true."

"How long have you been working here?"

"I've only just started."

"I've got a better job for you!"

Danilo was frightened that the stranger was testing him out on orders from Antoine. In the desire to find a better job, he could lose the one he had.

"If you're interested, of course!" the stranger repeated, looking him straight in the eye.

"What sort of job is it?" Danilo asked, more out of politeness than actually believing in the job.

"I've got an elderly relative who's lost the use of his legs. He doesn't see very well, either. His eyes are weak, and he likes to read, but he can't. I think he'd take to you very well. He's rich, but he's a good man, too. He's got a big house. You could live in. His name's Vogeler. Have you got a piece of paper? I'll write down the address."

Danilo went to the counter where he kept a small notepad. The sergeant never took his eyes off him. He was glad that Danilo and Rinaldo were not from the same area. He had already ascertained that Rinaldo was from Catalonia. Now that Danilo had confirmed that he was from Thrace, he realized that the two young men came from opposite ends of the earth. The sergeant was quite sure that Danilo and Rinaldo did not know each other. He had asked himself once again whether he had perhaps made a mistake. Now it was no longer important. The sergeant broke into a smile when Danilo came up and handed him the notepad.

Danilo was not to know that he would be under constant surveillance the moment he moved into old man Vogeler's house.

30
The Old Oak

THE NEXT DAY Danilo found himself in front of the gate to a huge walled mansion. The high wall was overgrown with ivy. The wrought iron gate was opened by a very neatly turned out, polite manservant. They started down a paved path. On both sides were birch trees, willows and some low unusual shrubs that Danilo had never seen before. They passed denuded chestnut trees and a small lake with a dried tree trunk sapling sticking out of it. The garden around the lake continued into a wood. Behind a bend in the path Danilo caught sight of an old three-floor stone house covered in creeper. It had a dark red tiled roof. This extremely well preserved building gave off an air of times past and utter calm.

Old man Vogeler sat in a wheelchair in front of the entrance, a smile on his face. He was wearing a dressing gown with a shawl round his shoulders. Danilo went up to him. Giving a courteous bow he greeted the gentleman who gave off the same air of calm and warmth as like his surroundings.

"Are you completely on your own in Rome, young man?"

"Yes, sir."

"That's a good thing. It makes a person strong. I heard that you're studying medicine."

"Well, I've enrolled. But I haven't managed to go to any lectures yet. I've been busy all the time. Struggling to earn a living."

"Well, you won't have too many duties in my house. You'll read to me from time to time. We'll talk. I'm getting old and like a bit of company. Come with me and I'll show you your room. You worked all night. You must be tired?"

"Yes, sir. Like a siren from space, as my boss, Antoine, would say," Danilo gave a smile.

Mr Vogeler introduced Danilo to the servants. The man who had received Danilo at the gate took him up to the attic and showed him his room. Then he withdrew without a word. Absolutely exhausted, Danilo threw himself onto the bed. He was calm, but he could not get to sleep. He had already forgotten that he was in Rome. His whole world was now narrowed down to this house and garden. Everything else beyond the wall seemed too far away. Vogeler's estate appeared enough for him. Stretched out on the bed, Danilo looked at the branches of an oak tree, which had become entangled in the upper windows. He knew that this old tree was part of the general atmosphere of tranquility. The stone mansion coexisted with the oak.

Danilo was relieved to feel that he had at last arrived in the right place. Working in the stables and at Antoine's was, in his view, aimless wandering.

Yet without this wandering he would not have ended up on the bed where he was now lying, tired out. The chirruping of birds came through the open window. Leaves rustled in the gentle breeze.

I love the sleep that autumn brings.
I love the way it penetrates my being, captures me, and carries me of so that I slowly sink, bit by bit, until the last points of light are extinguished in the darkness of my eyes.
And again the shapes of something important, something major elude me.
And I feel that it was just at this moment that I sensed them.

31
Letters Visible And Letters Invisible

NIGHT HAD FALLEN at the end of that day when Rinaldo came home tired from lectures. As he entered the house, he found a letter on the small table in the hall. He was taken aback. He had no one to write to him. He hurriedly opened the envelope. He saw a number of tattered pieces of paper. Among this heap, he caught sight of a letter written on clean white notepaper, as if it had been penned that same day. He recognized the unusual dialect, only used in the outlying regions of Galatia.

> Dear Sir,
>
> I regret that I did not have the opportunity to meet you personally. Nonetheless, I believe that the enclosed papers will interest you.
>
> Warm wishes and ΦΚΤ.

Rinaldo stared at the letter, puzzled. Suddenly he heard a sound behind him and raised his head. Mrs Shapiro emerged at the other end of the hall. She came towards him with a firm step.

"Rinaldo, please tell me how little Ari is getting on with his lessons."

She exuded a seductive scent. Rinaldo lowered his eyes from her bare shoulders to the bundle of papers. He was excited and could hardly wait to read them. Mrs Shapiro stood waiting for an answer. She slid the tips of her long soft fingers down his smooth neck.

"Not bad," Rinaldo smiled. "He still mixes up his Latin, though. Sitting with him, I'll soon forget myself what's correct and what isn't."

He stared at her long fingers. But his thoughts returned to the unusual writings he held in his hands. Her presence irritated him. He did not feel like chatting. He wished that she would finally turn round and go.

"I'm not so much concerned that he should learn how to use Latin correctly," said Natasha. "I'm anxious that he should develop a passion for searching. That he should learn to ask himself questions. You seem to be the only person he listens to." She fastened her large eyes on him with a clear gaze, full of trust.

Rinaldo wanted to be alone. "You're right, Madam. It would appear that only typists are able to learn the language as it should be used. The rest of us just stumble along and have a poor pronunciation."

A dark shadow flashed across her face. "There was something else I wanted to ask you. There will be a reception in this house next week. Many of my friends will come. I'd like you to be there, too."

"Of course. It would be an honor. Good night."

Natasha did not pursue the conversation. She felt sorry for Rinaldo, but at the same time, she admired him. She knew that he was more intelligent and able than all the other men she had ever known. Yet she also knew that Rinaldo was painfully lonely and that he considered himself the most worthless and unhappy of men.

Walking quickly, Rinaldo went to his room. He carelessly threw off his coat and sat down at his desk He had already forgotten Mrs Shapiro. He had also forgotten his fatigue and his lectures.

He lit two candles and put out the light. He then mumbled to himself for a long time in a mysterious voice as if saying an incantation. He covered the candle flames with the palms of both hands. When the strange prayer was over, he engrossed himself in the manuscripts. He started by noting down the characters that appeared most often. He returned to the beginning of the papers. He longed to decipher them. With blinding determination, with no thought for the passing of time, his eyes dilated, he stared at the indecipherable characters.

It was a windless night. There was no rustling of leaves. Only the barking of dogs in the distance disturbed this unnatural peace. At one moment, Rinaldo thought that the paper had a watermark. He held it up to the light of the flame. In vain. Nothing could be seen. All of a sudden, the empty white space between the lines started to darken. The effect of the heat made the invisible text in Galatian become clearer and clearer. A hidden message, written in white ink, rather like lemon juice, gradually unfolded in the candlelight.

Although I am a blind man, these are my words. They are genuine and were written with a goose feather from which all impurities were removed. In order for me to deceive my enemies, it may happen that nobody sees these words, just as I myself can no longer see them or read them. But if you, stranger, who read them are more cunning and more fortunate than I, go to Yellow Roses Street. At the entrance to number 32 ask for the good man Rami el Hassan. If he stays alive, he will show you my life's work among the books.

"How is that possible?" Rinaldo was amazed. The invisible letters are exactly in the middle of the spaces between the lines. A blind man could not have followed those lines when writing them. Someone must have read everything already. The visible, false letters were written in later as a form of protection. The secret message was hidden among the visible letters.

"Rinaldo, why are you always reading?" — a child's voice interrupted him.

Little Ari stood on the threshold of the half-illuminated room in the middle of the night. Rinaldo turned round suddenly. He looked like a faceless ghost. All that could be seen was the dark outline of his head. The feeble light flickered behind his back, but his face was in shadow. Neither his nose nor his eyes were visible, menacing from out of the darkness. He got up and went over to the terrified boy. Pulling him to his chest, he stroked his head.

"And why aren't you asleep, young man?"

"I was scared."

"Was it a nightmare? Did something wake you up?"

The boy clung even tighter to Rinaldo and nodded silently. Rinaldo gathered him up in his arms and took him to the room upstairs. He laid him down gently on the bed.

"Now we are both going to be quiet and listen to the night," whispered Rinaldo.

"I'm afraid of the night," Ari said.

"Why are you afraid of the night?"

"Because I dream about a lady."

"And is she ugly?"

"No. She's beautiful. She's even more beautiful than my mother. I'm not afraid. She wants to be kind to me and take me away. But I love my mother."

"She can't take you away, not when I'm here."

The boy did not reply.

"Don't be scared. Ill look after you and nothing can touch you. But now you must go to sleep. All good boys are asleep at this time of night."

Ari dutifully closed his eyes. Rinaldo stroked the boy's silky hair for a long time.

Rinaldo only returned to his room after Ari had fallen asleep. He sat down at his desk and picked up the papers. The letters he had seen but a short while before were no longer there. Horrified, he took his magnifying glass and examined the spaces between the lines. Not a sign, not a mark. There was nothing there. Between the mysterious, undecipherable characters there were just clean white spaces. It was as if the hidden text had been written in liquid with a short-term, self-destroying effect.

He brought the other text over to the flame. The secret letters did not appear. He grabbed another sheet but there was no change on that one either. The only thing that did happen was that the middle of the sheet scorched from being too close to the flame.

He had the impression that he was dreaming. He longer even himself believed that the hidden message had revealed itself. In a fit of rage, he screwed up the paper and threw it into the wastepaper basket.

32
Everything Will Come To An End Anyway

THE FOLLOWING MORNING, Rinaldo woke up with a headache. After discovering the hidden message, he could not get to sleep for a long time that night. He greeted the new day exhausted and short of sleep. But as soon as he saw the daylight, he immediately got up. He dressed hastily and had breakfast on the run. All the time his mind was occupied with how to reach Yellow Roses Street by the quickest route.

When he arrived at the address, Rinaldo remembered the day he had been released from prison. The ramshackle building that was number 32 looked in a far worse state than the building in Lutetia in which Kristina lived.

He went into the rundown hall. The smell of boiled cabbage filled the air. As he read the unknown names on the doors, he could not help thinking of Kristina. Even the most banal details unexpectedly rekindled unpleasant memories. He was torn between past and present. He looked for a door-plate with the name Rami el Hassan, yet constantly expected to read Kristina's name instead.

He knocked on a door with no name. The children's voices that had been audible from the apartment suddenly stopped. A few moments later, there came the sound of cautious footsteps. A dark-skinned foreigner appeared at the door.

"Are you Rami el Hassan?" asked Rinaldo.

Taken aback, the man stood in front of the half-open door. He wiped his mouth on his sleeve. He could not speak for surprise.

"I'm a friend of the blind Galatian," Rinaldo introduced himself.

"He wasn't blind!" exclaimed the man.

"Maybe he didn't tell you. His sight wasn't good."

Suspicious, Rami el Hassan shook his head.

"I got a letter!"

"A letter!" the man beamed. "I knew he was an honest man! I knew he'd write to you! Come in! Come in!"

Happy now, he waved the young man into the apartment.

"I've come for the books!" Rinaldo interrupted him.

"The books are down in the cellar. Come in and have a drink! We'll get the books later."

"I'm sorry, but I haven't got time!"

Muttering something to himself, the man went into the apartment. An inquisitive dark-eyed little girl soon poked her head through the half-open door. The Moroccan returned with a bunch of keys and a lighted candle. He led Rinaldo down a dark staircase. They went through a broken wooden door into the basement.

"Aren't you afraid of rats?" asked Rinaldo.

"Oh, no! Your friend's a good man. He poisoned them all!"

"Did he wash off the poison?"

"The whole room! We had to throw everything out because of the police. He's either writing or mixing powders. He did nothing else. Everyone thought he was mad. They called him Emperor of the Galatians."

"Why Emperor of the Galatians?"

"That's people for you! Evil-minded! As soon as a clever man appears, they laugh at him! Your friend was clever. I can vouch for that! It's a fact. He poisoned everything. Now there's not a single ant in the building, nor a single rat."

The Moroccan was in a good mood now. On the first landing the underground corridors forked. They went down some steps, to a second level, the lowest there was. Clutching the lighted candle, Rami el Hassan set off down the dirtiest corridor.

"It's like I'm back in prison," thought Rinaldo and shuddered.

The Moroccan stopped. Just before the end of the corridor. He pointed to a notice nailed to a door:

> Record No. K4223: Items related to compulsory eviction from the apartment on the second floor left and disposal of items and persons found therein.

When he turned the key in the rusty lock, they stepped into a cramped, stinking room piled up to the ceiling with things. The Moroccan set the candle down upright on a beam. He began to clear his way through the piles of sacks and boxes. Rinaldo took the dirty objects he handed him and put them down in the corridor. He thought he would choke with the dust. As he placed a smelly blanket on the floor, he recalled the prison again.

Finally, a worm-eaten chest bound with iron bands emerged. The Moroccan picked up and candle and lifted the lid.

"There are the books! The landlady wanted to burn them. Afterwards I lied to her that I that a thin man had given money for the books."

"What thin man?"

"The one who wrote you the letter. A good man. He's a Galatian, too, but he works too hard. I drove him in my cab. He came here and gave the landlady some money."

Rinaldo went up to the chest. As the Moroccan stood behind it, Rinaldo ran his hand over the books as if to convince himself that this was all real. He was horrified at the thought that he would have to put the books down on the damp floor. But he had no choice. He started to take them out. He didn't even look at the titles. He worked quickly trying to empty the chest as fast as possible.

"Now the landlady dare not burn anything," said the Moroccan. "I said that the thin man was a police spy."

"You mean, an inspector?"

"Yes, that. But she gets the message when something's dangerous."

Not turning towards the Moroccan, Rinaldo carefully went through the chest. He found nothing other than the ruined books. Disappointed, he regretted that he come on a fool's errand. He noticed a damaged page sticking out of one book. He opened the book mechanically to return the page. He could not believe his eyes. The book had a rectangle cut through all its pages. Putting his fingers in the hole, he felt a lead box concealed there. He did not dare take it out. His hands were shaking. He crouched beside the chest so that the Moroccan could not see anything. To avoid suspicion, he took another two books, beside the one with the piece cut out and placed them to one side.

"I'll take these three books as a keepsake," said Rinaldo, returning the others to the chest. "They'll all be ruined anyway!"

"You're right. These books are buried here in their own coffin."

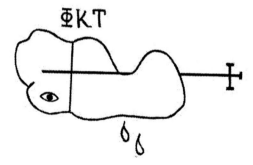

33
A Happy Childhood

Ten measures of wealth came down to earth
The Romans took nine, and left the tenth to the world.
Ten measures of wisdom came down to earth
The Jews took nine, and left the tenth to the world.

FOR DAYS JOSÉ ALKORTA spent all his time on preparations to found the University. He tried to postpone the rest of his duties. However, he could not get out of a visit to the newly-opened Jewish nursery school "Happy Childhood". Wherever they move in, the Jews first build a meeting-house, which they call a *Beth Knesset*. The Romans call it a synagogue and mistakenly think that it's just a place of worship. Beside the meeting-house, the Jews immediately erect a school and a kindergarten. Personally, the minister did not care much for nursery schools. But he knew that the Jews devote a lot of attention to their children's education. So this visit meant a lot to everyone, as a gesture of goodwill.

As soon as the Minister of Education, Mr José Alkorta, appeared accompanied by his secretary he became the centre of attention. He was surprised by the brightness of the pale colors that decorated the rooms. The sun smiled down from the wall, drawn with chubby cheeks and large laughing eyes. He stretched his dazzling rays as if wanting to embrace the world in his happiness. Beneath the sun, on the clean pale blue sky, little white clouds wearing colored caps were sailing along.

Little boys in sailor suits and little girls in white dresses caught three imaginary circles, one inside the other. As the game progressed, the living circles whirled in opposite directions until the children broke them up through their inelegant jumping. Holding hands with arms raised they converged towards the middle. Their laughter was followed up by a storm of clapping.

During the entertainment, the distinguished minister forced a smile at the invited guests, both Romans and Jews. He watched the children's show with disinterest and could hardly wait for it to finish. Suddenly the children broke into a counting rhyme:
"*En, den, di-nu,*"
The minister sat up with a start.
"*sa-va-ra-ka-ti-nu...*"
Totally serious, he turned to his secretary.
"Do you know this song?"
"First time I've heard it," said the woman surprised at the question.
"*sa-va-ra-ka-ti-ka-ta-ka...*"
José started to shiver. You could hear the children's laughter. It was a counting rhyme which the children used to sing in Galatia. He hadn't heard that song since his childhood.

Many Jews lived in harmony with the Galatians despite the fact that the Jews were a peace-loving nation and the Galatians a warlike race. Nevertheless, they shared common enemies so they used to perish together in wars. It was on account of or these misfortunes that the Galatians loved all Jews just as the Galatian Jews loved the Galatians. Perhaps this children's rhyme was a relic of their life together — José reflected. With swift strokes of his pen he wrote in his pocket diary: *Why savaraka?*

He was by now quite relaxed. He felt pleasant in these strange surroundings. He stood encircled by children and their mothers. They all laughed as one little boy shook the minister's trouser leg for the distinguished guest to pick him up. José held out his hand to the child. But at that very moment he saw a beautiful red-haired woman coming over to him with a bouquet of flowers in her hand. José bent to receive the flowers and kiss the woman as a mark of gratitude. The last thing he saw was the flash of a steel blade hidden among the blooms.

José fell to the ground face down. The small boy who had pulled his trouser leg finally managed to climb onto his back. He tugged at José's hair, wondering why he would not play with him. Blood spilled over the discarded knife and scattered flowers.

There was a scream.

34
Color Number Seventeen

THE MINISTER'S DEAD BODY lay on a wheeled bed covered by a dark green sheet. Beside the bed stood a medical examiner and his assistant. The doctor held a death certificate in his hand.

"Heart attack," he said coldly. "Chronic spasm of the coronary arteries."

The minister who had believed that all deaths were natural had died by a woman's hand. But because of high interests of state, the cause of death had to be altered.

The young assistant was writing furiously. The doctor lifted the sheet and exposed an inert head. They both gave a shudder. The dead man's face was smiling. His face muscles were as stiff as when he had bent down to receive the flowers. José smiled even in death.

The young man could not pull himself together. He tried to avert his eyes from the ghostly scene. In the cold mortuary the doctor's voice rang out:

"Teeth: color number seventeen. Number four upper left, caries…"

The assistant wrote it down. Completely thrown off balance by the dead man's smile, his thoughts in a jumble, he tried to recall the recently learned lesson about death halting the process of tooth decay. Teeth rot during life. After death, the body decomposes, but teeth are not subject to further change. After death, teeth are the most resistant part of the human body. Teeth are the decoration of a smile. And a smile was what decorated this deceased. But it was pointless! The assistant remained completed confused.

Careful examination revealed all the illnesses from which José had suffered. The Galatians are very like the Romans so, even in death, José did not give up the secret of his origin. Even his eyes, *post mortem*, took on a greenish-brown hue as was also usual in dead Romans.

The medical examiner would give the corpse a gentle tap on the joints with a silver gavel. At funerals it was the custom among the Romans that the high priest would gently tap the dead dignitary with a silver gavel three times on the forehead and call him by his given name. Engrossed in his notes, the young man jotted things down unconsciously expecting the sound of the deceased's name to ring out in the silence. The voice of the doctor cut in instead:

"Write this down! Request use of the refrigerator for two days."

As if to spite them, the dead minister continued to smile. At moments his eyes were lively and darting, like those of a squirrel. And he frequently spoke to himself.

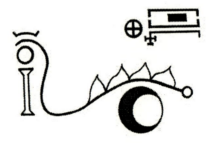

35
Accidental Death

**Here I, Vesko, lie beneath the earth
While you read this.
It would be better if I were reading
And you lying here.
*(Inscription on a wayside standing gravestone,
somewhere in the land of Galatia).***

THE MORNING WHEN IT broke was cold. After breakfast, Danilo read the news to old Vogeler as usual. As he opened the newspaper that day, his attention was drawn to a report from a court case dealing with the sale of state-owned mills. He resolved to skip that. His eyes skated over a huge advertisement for the sale of women's tights. The picture showing a beautiful pair of slim legs took up half a page. Then, between the ads and the debate on the water-mills, he caught sight of a banner headline:

DEATH OF IMPERIAL MINISTER FOR EDUCATION MR JOSÉ ALKORTA

As he read this out loud, he gave old Vogeler an excited look.
"That was me!" he cried out. "Mr Vogeler, that was me!"
The old man did not say a word. Quiet as ever, he bowed his head.
"Mr Vogeler, I wrote that report in the morgue! I saw that man. I saw that man when I was training in the mortuary."
The old man nodded to him to go on reading.
"During an official visit to the newly-built Happy Childhood nursery school the noble heart of imperial education minister Mr José Alkorta suddenly stopped. Following a heart attack, the minister was taken away by ambulance. On the way to hospital the vehicle, which was driving a

great speed, suddenly left the road for as yet unexplained reasons and hit a tree. After a hopeless struggle to save him, the number one man in the field of science and education died from his injuries later that night."

Danilo looked again at Vogeler. The man was silent. But his lower jaw seemed to start trembling.

"I saw with my own eyes that the minister had been stabbed through the chest with a knife" — Danilo was upset. — "It wasn't a heart attack! It was murder!"

"Perhaps he was only wounded in the nursery school," said the old man at last. "Yes. It is probable that he survived the knife attack. If he avoided the first death, then he died in the traffic accident as he was being driven to hospital!"

"The papers say it was an accident!"

"Yes, it's a damned riddle," Vogeler raised his voice. "He wasn't born by accident in order to die by accident."

"So it was murder then?"

"It was easy enough to fix. Loosen a screw in the wheel and there's your accident."

"Is that really possible?"

"This time it appears that it wasn't. I have the impression that nobody had reason to hate Alkorta. What would anyone gain by killing him? A new minister would only bring new misunderstandings. But you tell me this, Danilo, if a child is born blind, is he blind by accident or is he doing penance for somebody else?"

"I know! The answer is that it's the will of God!"

"But why does God want that?"

"That's not for us to know."

"And do you think we'll know why Alkorta died? All the forces of this world, my Danilo, have got mixed up. If the time is right, we can influence some of them. You told me that you directed all your strength towards getting yourself out of the desert. Do you think that that major appeared just by chance? Your unfortunate group leader certainly thinks so."

"Everything you say fits in with the teaching of ancient peoples that nothing happens by chance and that is destined to fulfill some mission in life."

"Just keep your eyes open! Every apparently unimportant detail, every coincidence, is a sign. It must have happened to you that you did something and that you repeated the same mistake several times in a row. That could have been a signal to you to stop what you were doing on the spot. Maybe you should have been in quite another place at that moment. A gardener, if he breaks his hoe twice in a row, finds something else to do that day."

"And if we don't take note?"

"Nothing happens! You've missed the sign. Then next time the major won't appear to bail you out."

"But I haven't received any such sign up to now."

Old man Vogeler smiled gently. "Perhaps you just didn't notice it just as you didn't notice a dead minister lying beside you!"

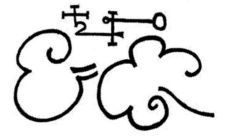

36
Double Death

THE WRETCHED MINISTER seemed to be fated to die that day. He could not avoid a double death. If he had survived the stab wound, he would have been killed in the traffic accident while being driven to hospital. With the circumstances being so entangled, the exact cause of the minister's death could not be determined. But then that didn't really interest anyone very much. A heart attack as the official cause of death suited everyone.

If José had died in Galatia, his body would be laid out on a bier in an open wooden coffin, decorated with a wreath of wild flowers. In that wilderness, the people believe that every family has its own celestial domestic protector whose blessed visage painted on a wooden board hangs on the wall of the largest room in the house. When household members are born or die, the wooden image is taken down and placed at the head of the cradle or coffin. Although the priests forbid this, ahead of the funeral the uneducated peasants secretly put money into the pockets of the deceased to have with him handy for life in some other world. Unfortunately, the high position in society that José held threw this all into confusion. Roman dignitaries wear ceremonial silk suits with sewn up pockets and it is in these suits that they are buried. Nor are the coffins kept open, as is the custom with superstitious peoples whom the Romans ridicule, saying that they idolize wooden boards.

Mr José Alkorta ended life as a Roman. With no money for the afterlife, no heap flowers and no painted icon which had marked his birth.

The cemetery for distinguished citizens was closed to the public that day. As the weather was cold, the only uninvited guest was a dark-skinned man, who was shabbily dressed. The stewards removed him immediately. In the presence of the highest-ranking servants of the empire, the coffin was draped in a blue flag with the eagle and the cross.

From the hearse, soldiers carried the coffin on their shoulders to the official catafalque. Beneath their black blankets the horses shivered with the cold. There came the sound of the dead march and cannon salutes. The invited dignitaries gathered around the coffin where they read pre-prepared speeches and expressed their condolences.

Vicena stood to one side as usual. He gazed scornfully upon the small-time glory-hunting bureaucrats. They enjoyed funerals, which afforded them the opportunity to suck up to some bigwig or other. In normal circumstances they had no chance of getting near Roman ministers, let alone talking to them. In this melee Vicena noticed the head of the Registry Department approaching him. The mealy-mouthed requests of this toad disgusted him.

"Minister, we have run into a problem."

"My dear chap, we all run into problems," replied Vicena.

"This matter is very serious!" he whispered "We can't enter Mr Alkorta into the Register of Deaths."

Vicena gave him a suspicious look. Flustered, the department head looked around him cautiously. He continued in a low voice:

"Mr Alkorta died twenty years ago! As a young man!"

Vicena was beginning to lose his temper.

"This is hardly a time for jokes!"

"There's no mistake, Minister! I know what I'm saying!"

Vicena stared at him in absolute amazement. The department head continued:

"The Alkorta who died twenty years ago had the same birth certificate as the Alkorta who has just died now."

"What about the parents?" Vicena asked.

"The entire family died the same day."

"Yes, Alkorta had lost his parents, was an orphan."

"He wasn't an orphan! They all died the same day! He and his parents!"

"Listen, man!" Vicena's patience was really being tried. "Who thought up this trick?"

"Nobody knows. It all seems incredible! As if the bogus Alkorta had used the birth certificate of the real Alkorta, who was long dead. On the basis of that birth certificate he could get hold of all other necessary documents."

"I don't understand," Vicena interrupted, "why you keep trying to cover up the mistake your service made with these stupid fairy tales! We all know that Alkorta lost his parents early in life. The fact that your inefficient clerks had him down as dead is no reason for us to be fooling around now with these idiotic stories. You should be ashamed of yourself!"

The department head was speechless, his mouth agape. Vicena went on in a threatening tone:

"José Alkorta has died now! As for that cock-up of twenty years ago, deal with it as best you can! Don't let me have to send in my men to sort it out!"

"Perhaps it would be best if we put them down as brothers? Twin brothers?"

But Vicena had already turned his head away, without answering. The department head once again turned about him in fear. Trying to remain unnoticed, he left that group and hurried back to his office.

It was now Vicena's turn to pay his last respects to the dead minister. With tired, clumsy steps, almost staggering, he approached the catafalque. He cast another glance at those present and placed his left hand on the silk flag draped over the coffin. With the tips of his short, podgy fingers, he tapped the coffin lid through the flag.

"My dear friend! I called you José. No elevated forms of address, no official titles. I admired your simplicity and warmth. But it is only today, now that you have gone, that I appreciate your wisdom. Just as the delicate rose protects itself from pests with its thorns, so wise men protect themselves from fools with foolishness. In these dark times, the New University, which is the result of your effort, will light the way for new, more educated generations. When our planet becomes greener, as you so eloquently put it, people will understand the benefit you brought. It was through you that the University was inaugurated. No one will be fully aware of all that you did. Nor the measures you had resort to in order to deceive your friends and enemies and achieve your goal. My dear friend, rest in peace! In the place where no one has a name!"

"Rest in peace!" chorused those present.

At a sign from Vicena, they pulled the flag away. They lowered the coffin carefully on ropes down into the grave. The first handful of greasy black earth banged onto the shiny polished lid. The sound of muttered prayers for the dead was heard, along with the snorting of frozen horses. There was a cold wind blowing. And everything came to an end swiftly as no one felt like hanging around the cemetery for long.

Emperor Bonifacio was absent due to illness. He took José's death to be a bad omen. In his grief, he was worried and ill-tempered over the coming days. It was known that the emperor did not like appointments and did not take kindly to new people in his vicinity. They could not even replace court servants when one of them died or left, let alone an eccentric minister whom the emperor himself always seemed to protect.

It was freezing outside. Tiny, dirty snowflakes had started to fall. Mr Alkorta was no longer alive.

On his way home in a Roman suburb, the dark-skinned man, frozen to the marrow, told his wife that a friend had died. He had recognized José's face in the papers and realized that the dead minister was none other than the Galatian to whom he had given the letters. He recalled the story told by his long deceased neighbor that the souls of Galatians wander for forty days after their death, tortured by hunger and an unquenchable thirst. That is why family members leave out food and water on the table. What use were cannon salutes to the poor minister when he was a Galatian. What a waste, all the honors and pictures in the papers, when he was now having a hard time.

At family lunch, on the worm-eaten shaky table, there was a tin plate containing cooked rice, placed to one side, which no one touched. The hungry children quickly ate up their portions and did not even notice the plate.

Death alone forces people to reflect on life. But even then the reflection is half-hearted and reluctant. For the rest, many Romans were now convinced that life in the city was going on just as before, as if the skinny minister had never existed.

As a sign of respect, flags were flown at half-mast. Mr José Alkorta, imperial minister of education, was buried with all honors and no one grieved.

37
The Secret Of Dead And Living Words

VICENA CLUTCHED JOSÉ'S POCKET DIARY BETWEEN his short fat fingers. A little bag lay open on the desk with a tag, which said *Working Case C-KC 7371/6*. Laid out beside the bag were a ring, two medals, some keys, several sheets of writing and receipts for paid bills. The entire worldly belongings of Mr Alkorta, neatly marked and inventoried, barely covered the desk.

"Now we'll find out finally why you came to see me!" Vicena murmured with excitement. "Then you spoke to me of poisoning. You asked for a list of students. You were alive then and thought you could put one over on me. But now you're dead. Now we'll see what it was you were hiding."

Vicena took his own diary out of his pocket and placed it on the desk beside José's. He followed every line of his notes with the tip of his forefinger. When he came upon the day of José's last visit, he picked up José's diary. He leafed through it carefully twice as if unable to believe his eyes. The page with the date he was looking for had been torn out. And after the ripped out page, the diary was completely blank. From that date on, José had not written down anything up to the day he was killed. He had not even recorded the opening of the University. No meetings, no official duties concerned him any longer. Only the last two words remained:

Why savaraka?

With a slow movement, as if trying to conceal his disquiet even from himself, Vicena put his own and José's diaries into a drawer. Then he picked up the notebooks from the desk. Try as he might, he could not read the writings there. All the pages had been written in short, unconnected words. People who ridicule words cannot even begin to imagine how each written word can also serve as a reminder. With its enormous strength, every word hid within itself whole events in condensed form, memories and decisions. It had been enough simply for José to look at the notebook and form complete pictures from the curved letters of a single word. The words written down there were dead. Precisely that. When José died, the damned words died with him.

In a bad mood, Vicena prepared to lay aside the useless notebooks. All the time he could think of nothing but the last two words.

"Why savaraka?" — he was puzzled. "What's that supposed to mean?"

Vicena had long been convinced that José was hiding something. The Minister of Education had managed to deceive all those around him until his last day on earth, when he forgot. Something had been stronger than his caution. And that something had cost him his life.

Suddenly, a bit of paper fell out of the notebook. Vicena clumsily tried to catch it in mid-air, but failed. As soon as the paper alighted on the floor, Vicena put his foot on it. Filled with excitement, he quickly bent down as if afraid the piece of paper might fly away. From the floor he picked up a post office receipt for a registered letter. Written on the receipt in José's handwriting were Rinaldo's name and his address.

"You're cunning, my friend," he muttered. "Or rather, you *were* cunning. But as you see, there are people smarter even than you!"

Truth to tell, José would never have left such a trail behind him. In his time, he wanted to send the letter to Rinaldo by post and receive confirmation that the communication had been delivered. That is why he used the special pre-paid service. It was unfortunate that the confirmation had come when José was already dead.

"You knew everything. Except when you were going to die!"

Vicena's face was radiant. Rinaldo's name and address were the clue, which would lead to a solution. It seemed that he would have no trouble in concluding the investigation.

In only a few hours he drew up a complete report on Rinaldo. Vicena had held his breath when he took hold of the papers. In his hands he held a copy of the special 30-day authorization that he had given José. It was on the basis of this authorization that the order had been issued to release Rinaldo from prison. Vicena found it hard to compose himself.

In his hands he held the authorization he had signed when José had come for the list of students. He broke out in a sweat as he realized that in signing it he had involved himself.

"This is a real conspiracy!" — it took his breath away. "So that's why you tricked me, my friend? Why? You scared me with that poisoning story, and all the time you were bringing suspicious characters to Rome."

He stared at the photograph of the unknown youth for a long time, as if wanting to commit to memory every single feature. He had not taken to Rinaldo the first time he saw him. His face, stiff as that of a stuffed cat, had given nothing away. Rinaldo had looked like a man completely closed in on himself. Vicena hated having anything to do with such, as he saw it, dishonest and dangerous types. He put the photograph in his jacket pocket and again took the report from the Recruiting Office. He read it carefully endeavoring to memorize each word.

An extremely talented person. Seriously ill. His difficulty in establishing relationships with those around him makes him unsure when drawing the line between the real and unreal world. There is a latent danger of audio hallucination. Illness: schizophrenia; clear autistic behavior. He sees any personal experience as a result of the violent influence of some cosmic, supernatural force. Through hypnotic suggestion, these forces direct his thoughts and actions. Unsuitable. Shoot in time of war!

Vicena was puzzled. He became aware that he had liked José and could not reconcile himself to the fact that his friend had deceived him. He was not so much hurt by the thought of a possible conspiracy as by this betrayal of trust. He was calmed by the reflection that José and Rinaldo probably did not know each other. Once again he took the photograph out of his pocket. Once again he carefully went over every detail of Rinaldo's face.

"So you're haunted by visions, are you!" he muttered. "For the moment, it's pictures, and soon it'll be sounds, too! You're sick, and, therefore, dangerous. But don't worry; we'll help you not to do anything foolish!"

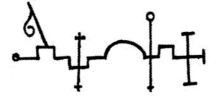

38
Fire Spots

ON THE EVE of her reception, Mrs Shapiro looked more beautiful than ever. Her eyes were restless and clear like those of young girl, but they commanded respect like those of a wise man. She was good at listening to people without interrupting them. Her face would mirror the deep pain or great joy she shared with the person talking.

"Come on, young Rinaldo! Don't start pussyfooting now. They've all arrived. Just tidy your hair up a bit."

With her fingertips she gently touched his head. Suddenly she withdrew her hand. Their confused glances met. They stood like that for a moment, trembling. Her slim figure and lovely long legs were outlined by the clinging dress. A passionate, binding force drew them towards each other. Rinaldo had the impression that he already held her firm, naked body in his arms. He almost kissed her with his half-open lips.

"It's madness, Rinaldo!" she pulled away.

After a moment where she was intoxicated by his magic touch, she seemed resolute once more.

"Come on, young man! The guests are arriving."

Mrs Shapiro shepherded the budding physician into a large salon. Inside, in small groups, stood people wearing expensive clothes and jewelry to show their standing and their power. Following short introductions, Rinaldo was ushered into a rather noisy group. Although he did not drink, he casually held a glass of pungent sparkling wine in his hand.

"Yes. I heard the story of Manolo the builder when I was governor of Athens," one guest was bragging. "Athens is truly one of the world's most beautiful cities!"

"Still, I'll tell the story for those that don't know it," the thin man with the goatee beard persisted.

"That story's a real bore!" opposed the governor, visibly hot under the collar.

"You're wrong!" the thin man interrupted him. "That story's gives a picture of real life."

The rest of the group gave approving nods of heads, eager to hear the story that had made the governor get so upset.

"Manolo and his men were building a tower. And everything they put up during the day, they would pull down at night. The men would long build the villa and then demolish what they'd done. Until Manolo announced that he'd had a vision that the tower would only be finished when they'd walled up a live woman in its foundations."

"I think they have a similar story in Moldavia," a rather ugly man tossed into the conversation.

Ignoring this remark, the man with the goatee continued:

"Manolo recounted his dream to the others. They decided to sacrifice the woman or sister who was the first to bring them food and water the following day. They swore to each other not to say a word about this arrangement, but to come to work next day and wait. But what do you think happened? All the builders except Manolo ordered their wives not to visit them the following day at all costs. Only Manolo kept his word. The next day his wife appeared bringing food. While she was still thinking it was all a joke, stone blocks crushed her body. That was the price Manolo paid to finish the tower."

"That's not the way to tell it!" the governor broke in. "There's a lot of poetry in that story. You haven't a clue!"

"No, no! It's not about an individual. The story tells of progress and how in achieving progress the little man always has to suffer."

"And just where do you see progress there?" the governor rudely interrupted him.

"The tower represents progress. It had to be built. And for that to be done a price had to be paid!" the governor countered.

"And why did it have to be built? Because the ruler who had commissioned it had threatened to execute all the masons if it wasn't! Why didn't Manolo kill himself? In that way he'd have saved his wife, who was also pregnant, by the way. Quite simply, Manolo was determined the build the tower."

"But what you're saying is awful! You are twisting a great story."

"I also think it's a great story! But I also think that for Manolo the tower was more important than his wife. Otherwise, he'd have told her not to come to the building site. Would you, sir, sacrifice everything to build the tower of your dreams? Would you go so far as to sacrifice your wife and unborn child?"

"You can't go against well-known facts," the governor grumbled. "The story presents the masses."

"Modern medicine," added another guest, "absolutely rejects these visionary dreams."

Now all the others, up to then disinterested listeners, joined in the heated debate. Rinaldo withdrew. He did not like battles of wits. He examined those present carefully. They were elegant and much older than he was. But in the other half of the room his eyes fell on a beautiful girl. The next moment, however, he lost sight of her among the crowd of other guests.

"I don't think the masses can live without progress!" The debate on Manolo was still going on.

Trying to catch a glimpse of the beautiful girl, Rinaldo's eyes met those of Mrs Shapiro. She was watching the servants and gauging the mood of her guests. She saw Rinaldo standing there on his own. Resolute and laughing, she made towards him. Standing there like a wallflower, he was spoiling her reception. Sensing her intention, the young man beat her to it and rejoined the first group. The subject of conversation had changed.

"My dear chap, these winters are getting worse and worse," the governor was explaining.

"It's no wonder His Imperial Majesty is ill."

"They're right when they say the sun is cooling down," the governor went on. "For as long as I can remember, each winter has been worse than the one before! We'll soon have snow falling in summer."

"And if it's as cold as this in Rome, what must it be like in the mountains of the north?"

Rinaldo suddenly felt a pain in his head. Putting both hands to his forehead, he moved away from the group. He half-closed his eyes. In an effort to remain calm, he pressed his palms hard against his temples. The pain eased in a trice. He breathed a sigh of relief. This time he resolved to stay on his own. He felt he had to get out of this strange hubbub as soon as he could.

"And I saw you, too, Rinaldo," — he was stopped in his tracks by a tender female voice behind him.

He turned sharply. He saw the blonde hair and innocent eyes from his dream. The girl was standing there confidently. Her face exuded the beauty of a contented woman.

"Kristina!" he said breathlessly. "I've been looking for you for ages. I'm still hopelessly in love with you!"

"And I loved you, Rinaldo. But you were always in love with yourself, not with me!"

"I still love you! Even more than before!"

"There's no hope left for us now. It's too late."

"Kristina, there's always hope!"

"Rinaldo, my husband is here."

"That's impossible!"

"I loved you a lot, too, Rinaldo. But you wanted to ruin me with your crazy love."

"Kristina, they took me away. I didn't..."

"Rinaldo, those are just words!"

At that moment who should come to them but the unpleasant man with the goatee beard.

"Sir," he bowed to Rinaldo contemptuously, barely concealing his laughter. "My wife has told me about you. Allow me to introduce myself. I'm Johannes Dirken, Kristina's husband and the father of her children."

Rinaldo gave a nod in greeting. Kristina was silent.

"Mrs Shapiro told me that you are studying medicine." The stranger's voice echoed in his ears. "You were there when we told the story of Manolo. I'm very interested to hear what you think?"

"I know a similar story from Serbia about the building of the town of Skadar."

"But this was no ordinary construction!" Johannes laughed again. "You are studying at the moment. You are giving up the best years of your life for the general good, as they say. At first glance, a modest existence and a lot of sacrifice. But then there follows a well-paid job and social prestige. Now you fight among yourselves like starving wolves for a scholarship or perhaps some award or other. You package your greed in the gift wrap of human welfare. But in essence, all those scientific debates and discoveries of yours are the result of a blinding instinct for self-proclamation. You are all like Manolo the builder. You would trample dead bodies just to attain your own selfish goals."

Kristina was still silent. Her rich platinum necklace set off her soft, smooth, pampered skin.

Rinaldo found it very difficult to compose himself. He tried to marshal his thoughts. Johannes had the better of him. As soon as the attack had begun, Rinaldo felt the ground slipping from under his feet. He was consumed with the horror of impotence. Johannes gazed at him with his cold, snakelike eyes.

"Hold your peace, young man! Don't say a word! You yourself know full well how morally decayed you scientists are. Your efforts are nothing more than slavish labour for selfish gain."

"I don't know. It's…" Rinaldo could not stand up to him. He was beaten.

"Yes! It is work, full of sweat. When did you ever hear that wise men work? Read the New Testament, read learned books. If people stopped working, there would be perfect peace and prosperity on earth. Work offends the Lord!"

There was no answer. The mocking smile Johannes gave spread all over his face. He knew he had broken his opponent. His eyes narrowed with hate. He was making fun of Rinaldo in front of Kristina.

A dull pain seized Rinaldo. His eyes clouded over. Faces became distorted. Things lost their shape. In a split second he recovered.

"Sir, it is written in the New Testament…"

"What is written, young man?" said Johannes triumphantly, preparing to deliver the final blow. "That elbow-pushers will occupy high positions? Young man, work is for idiots, not wise men!"

The pain became grew in intensity. Rinaldo started to feel completely disoriented from the sickening bouts of giddiness. His body jerked in spasms. He felt he was falling out of the saddle. He tried to grab the horse's mane. He felt a tremendous blow, as if stabbed in the leg. Sparks of fire showered in the dark sky. In the haze he saw the face of the skinny Minister of Education illuminated by fire. To his left and right, two men held the bunch of papers the minister had read. A blue flame burned in his eye sockets. Losing consciousness, Rinaldo heard his own voice coming out of the fire:

"No, sir. It is written there that wisdom justifies its own works. Without works, sir, there can be no wisdom."

The face of Johannes darkened. There followed an embarrassing silence. Kristina still said nothing. In any case, she was no paying attention to the confrontation.

The room turned on its head. Rinaldo saw all the objects about him duplicate and whiz around. He closed his eyes, trying to beat this thing off. The bodies of the guests changed shape, transforming themselves into dark riders. Rushing up into the heavenly heights, in the total pandemonium, ghostly winged horses whinnied. The air was in a whirl. The sound of horses' hooves drowned out the storm. A bloodstained flag unfurled amid the clouds. Ravens gathered round the heads of the horsemen, croaking. Alongside the company of riders wild dogs rushed, biting at their down-turned tails.

Heaven was all of a clamor, while utter peace reigned on earth. A thick dark fog fell upon the ground, extinguishing the day. Above the heavy layers of cloud, invisible to the human eye, the sky was red and stretched to infinity. Disease spread over the land and crops. Horned livestock fell prey to boils and anthrax. Tiny drill-shaped creatures entered their bodies through the sores. The swollen carcasses of the dead cattle were left to rot, unburied. The winter wheat was attacked by frost and froze. People died from infections. Only the red poppies remained to flower in spring.

As they galloped, the riders unsheathed their swords. The sharp blades flashed. The great dogs gave out bloodcurdling howls like wolves. It seemed that some hero had stepped out to prevent the onslaught. The black birds swooped down on him to peck him to death. The beating of wings and the cawing was mixed with the barking of the dogs.

Down on earth it was still quiet. The frost took hold, so violently that even rocks started to crack.

In their onrush, waving their swords, the accursed horsemen swooped down to trample the white rider and his mount. While he awaited them, rooted to the spot, without flinching. He tightened his grip on his sword. All of a sudden, he dug his spurs into his horse and charged the attackers. The dull sound of horses' hooves turned to thunder. Flames whirled out of the hooves. The leader of the horsemen brandished his sword. The sky broke up. The earth shook. As they clashed, the hoarse voice of Johannes resounded:

"Aha! Your friend is not so naïve, after all! But he is sad tonight. Yes, that's it exactly. Your friend is sad tonight, Kristina." Johannes put his arm round his wife's waist. Snuggling up to her husband, Kristina remained silent.

"Your friend looks as if he has tears in his eyes, Kristina," the words came. "He could start crying any moment!"

From a distance, Natasha Shapiro was following what was going on out of the corner of her eye. Kristina and Johannes were standing motionless in front of Rinaldo and looking at him inquisitively.

"Your friend is lonely!" Johannes' voice rang out loudly, as if it was speaking from Rinaldo's head. A second, female, voice started to laugh. "He's sad because he has no one to love."

"Excuse me, sir," Rinaldo scarcely got the words out. "I don't feel well. It was nice meeting you."

Restraining his pain, he gave a slight bow. As soon as he had left the big room, full of people, the voices subsided and stopped torturing him. With quick steps he made towards his room.

When he got finally back to his own world, he knelt on the floor and pressed his forehead against his knees. He was breathing with difficulty. Then he got up. Throwing his head back, he kept his eyes half-shut for some time. His jaw was locked in a vice. At last, his face muscles relaxed.

"Lord of the world, why have you abandoned me? Why have you given my enemies greater strength than mine? Have pity on me! Grant me mercy and I will glorify you more ardently than before! I give you my heart, my stomach! I give you all of me! Do not leave me disgraced before my enemies!"

Tears obscured his vision. And his words were mixed with sobs.

"Lord of the world, hear my lamentation! Lord of the world, look upon me! I must be strong!"

With clenched teeth and fists, Rinaldo collapsed on the bed. As a result of the long and painful spasms, all his strength had left him. The muffled sound of female giggling drifted in from the reception salon.

Midnight had long since passed. A full moon could be seen through the window. Its cold light illuminated the objects in the room. For a brief moment, memories of the night in prison when he had wakened in the middle of the night were brought to life. Exhausted, he could barely control his thoughts. He started at the thought of the dirty yellow light. His eyes ached. He could not sleep at night. Now he was finally at peace. And the soporific, unclear, low murmur of the guests somewhere in the distance sent the weary Rinaldo to sleep.

At one point during the night he felt a warm woman's body next to his. Everything was quiet. After the guests had departed, she had lain down and snuggled up to the young man. She threw a smooth, beautifully shaped leg across his knees and kissed him with passion and gentleness. Dazed with fatigue, he looked at her skin glowing in the moonlight. He buried his face in the auburn scented hair, as though seeking sanctuary. He caressed her gently in his delight. And lost in admiration, he kissed her breasts over and over again. She responded, pressing herself against him and trembling. Her body arched and she surrendered completely.

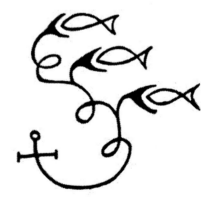

39
An Unknown Scent

WHEN RINALDO AWOKE, Natasha Shapiro had already risen. The hired maids were cleaning the house in the aftermath of the reception. Wearing a dressing-gown, Natasha was standing by the stove boiling some milk. She did not notice Rinaldo coming down the hall towards her. She was lost in thought, her eyes fixed on the saucepan to make sure the milk did not boil over.

Walking on tiptoe, Rinaldo noiselessly crept up behind her. He gently encircled her waist with his arms and kissed her behind the ear. Eyes half-closed, he sank his face into her long blonde hair. Pressing her trembling stomach with down-turned palms, he drew her to him. Her firm curves pressed against his body.

"Don't, Rinaldo!" she broke away.

Natasha's cheeks were burning as if someone had slapped her face. Rinaldo stepped back in amazement. The scent of her hair was quite different from the night before.

"Rinaldo, this isn't right. Please don't take advantage of my weakness. Your youth had me spellbound for a moment. An aroused urge beyond my control. I think it best that we forget about all this. Please, Rinaldo. For both our sakes."

She stopped, embarrassed. She tried to force a smile, but her face went stiff instead. She looked Rinaldo straight in the eyes.

At that moment, the milk boiled over.

Natasha, quite calm, took a cloth out of a drawer. She moved the saucepan aside and turned off the stove. She turned to face Rinaldo again.

"Anyway, Ari and I are leaving tomorrow to go on our annual vacation. We'll spend three weeks in the mountains, up north. I need some fresh air. When we come back, everything will be all right again, won't it?"

The stench of burnt milk filled the kitchen. Rinaldo made no reply. In his confused mind, he could not stop thinking about Natasha's completely different scent.

"Everything will be all right again?"

"Yes," Rinaldo nodded his head absently. "Everything will be like it was before."

He left the kitchen crushed. The stink of the burnt milk spread down the hall and irritated his nostrils. Rinaldo was no longer capable of recalling the gentle female scent which had thrilled him the whole night.

That day, Natasha was preoccupied with her own disjointed thoughts and failed to notice that the hired staff were moving about the house a little too easily, as if they already knew the layout of the rooms. She did not see one maid go into Rinaldo's room as soon as he left it. Cleaning that room had not been on the agenda, but nobody paid any attention to this error. When Rinaldo returned later, the bed was made, the curtains drawn aside, the window open and the wastepaper basket emptied.

40
Tale Of A Beautiful Witch

**The dragon stood before the woman
who was about to bear a child,
so that he might devour her child as soon as it was born.
(The Revelation to John, 12.4)**

MID-WAY THROUGH WINTER, the cold relented. But instead of the expected sunny days, a period of cold rains ensued. Danilo and old man Vogeler passed their time in the study, a bright room with large windows looking out over the garden. For the first time in his life, Danilo fastened his attention on the world around him. He was filled with happiness at his new life. The old gentleman was a wonderful teacher and a good master. They would spend hours in silence, and hours chatting.

One morning, there was a real downpour. You could not see through the window panes for the water that was pouring down them. The old man and the youth sat in silence, listening to the sound of the rain.

"Mr Vogeler, is there a God?" Danilo asked out of the blue.

The old man raised his gentle eyes. He was looking somewhere over the head of the young man. He smiled.

"There is for a believer!"

They fell silent again. The raindrops beat monotonously on the window panes and ran down the misted glass. There was a roaring fire in the room. Danilo broke the silence:

"According to the teaching of our state, God exists and before Him there was nothing. God created the world in six days and on the seventh he enjoyed what he had created. That's why a week has seven days."

"But why seven? Why not, for example, eight or ten?"
"I'd never thought of that!" said Danilo perplexed.
"Because people can only live in seven-day periods!"
Danilo stared at him wide-eyed. The old man went on in a quiet voice:
"The seven-day week was established long before we can even imagine. At a time when the measurement of time was linked to the story of the gods."
"But our state teaches us that there is only one master of the universe and that he created it."
"But where does that teaching come from? Our state simply took it over from former states. And those states, in the same way, from even older states. In time the story changed. The oldest legends tell of evil gods who already existed when our God, whose name we glorify, appeared. The story changed because new states emerged with the passage of time. And one of them needed a doctrine about a single good god. The story of that god was linked to the story of the week of seven days."
"Couldn't the number of days in the week be changed?"
"No! There were dictators and evildoers who laughed at those stories. They introduced ten-day weeks for their subjects and completely new calendars and names for the months, just in order to mock the good God. But they did not succeed. As I said already, people can only live in seven-day weeks. Nowadays we laugh at those stupid calendars, but not at the good God."
"But how did the evil gods disappear?"
"The evil gods continued to exist. In time, legend accorded them the role of the disobedient servants of the good God who punished them."
"That means, then, that the good master of the universe created something that was not good?"
"And not only that! The worst of all was Lilith."
"Lilith? I've never heard that name."
"Neither could you have done. No one wants to speak her name! In the teachings it says that God created her as He created Adam, from the earth. She was Adam's first wife. She was beautiful because God created her in His own image. Even the angels were captivated by her beauty and at the outset began to bow to her, thinking that she was God. But she did not want to remain in Paradise and go on living with Adam. One

day, she vanished, uttering an unpronounceable name. God sent three angels to search for her. They did not find her until they reached the Red Sea. But she refused to return. She was punished by being sentenced to devour one hundred children every day. It was only then that God created a second woman, Eve. Not from the earth this time, but from one of Adam's ribs."

"Why then does everyone keep quiet about Lilith? If she is a devil, then she's certainly weaker than her Creator!"

"That's precisely the trouble. She devours children. And who punished her in that way? None other than the good Lord himself. If it weren't for that punishment, Lilith would not have committed evil acts."

"Then our state is based on lies! It's all an underhand trick! Who can we trust?"

"Don't trust people!" replied the old man.

41
A Place Where The Dead Talk

RINALDO HAD BEEN FEELING unwell ever since Natasha and Ari set off on their holiday in the northern mountains. The house felt empty. As if he was living with ghosts. He was filled with disquiet until he finally summoned up the courage to enter the room where the reception had been held. He thought was seeing Kristina again. Johannes' voice still rang in his ears. He went up to the table over which Natasha's dressing gown had been thrown. She was wearing it the morning he had embraced her in the kitchen. He had never believed in the power of objects. But Natasha's dressing gown excited him more and more. He ran his hand over its soft material. He picked it up and sniffed it. He was horrified to realize that, instead of Natasha's scent, all he could smell was the stench of burnt milk.

He was obsessed with a kaleidoscope of unreal emotions in a room where he was quite alone. It was as though all the impressions were crowding in on him at the same time and with the same intensity. The scent of the dressing gown, Johannes' voice, Kristina's smile, the scalded milk, and Natasha's firm body. His only wish was to leave the room as soon as he could.

"I'm sick!" — he tortured himself with the thought. "It's as if someone has put curse on me!"

Preoccupied with these depressing thoughts, he returned to his room and lay down on his bed.

His thoughts went unconsciously towards the box found in the cellar in Yellow Roses Street. He looked towards the wardrobe in which he had put it. Then he jumped up with a start. On the door of the upper part of the wardrobe was a piece of broken wax. Ari was too small to reach that high. Natasha would never have taken the liberty of rummaging through someone else's belongings. The broken piece of wax, which had been placed in a visible spot, confirmed that somebody had gone through his things. He opened the wardrobe door. He broke out in a cold sweat when inside, beside the neatly ironed and stacked pillow cases and sheets, there was nothing. Someone had removed the box with the poison. He searched through the tidy pile of bed-linen. In vain. From the moment he had found the box in the cellar, Rinaldo had feared that someone might uncover its existence. The same Roman laws applied equally to murderers and those who made up poisonous substances. Under these laws, it was a highly punishable offence even to be in possession of poison. Nervous now, Rinaldo thought back to the hired servants who had moved so knowingly through the apartment. One of them knew that the box was to be sought in the wardrobe.

All his books and papers had been moved. The wastepaper basket was still empty. His glance came to rest on the three books, brought from the cellar. They stood on the shelf. Judging by the trail of dust on the shelf beneath the books, someone had taken them down. Obviously the person had not considered them of any importance, and had put them back in their place.

Rinaldo was at a loss what to do. He hoped that in the haste of the search, No one had noticed that one book had been cut into. He took down all three books. He had to get rid of them.

He decided to go out into the city. He could not regain his composure however he tried. He was comforted by the thought that only the possession of dangerous, that is, fatal poisons was punishable by law. For days now he had been trying, unsuccessfully, to discover the composition of the powder in the box he had found. On the basis of its smell, he concluded that musk was the strongest constituent in the powder. However, after the mess up with the scalded milk, he could no longer trust to his sense of smell. He doubted that a blind man would call a standard poison his life's work. Rinaldo hoped that the box contained some sort of medicine or opiate, which the law tolerated.

He could not stop thinking about where he might hide the books. He did not dare to throw them away just like that as he might need them. In this upset state, he walked about for sometime hoping that this would have a calming effect. He frequently turned to look behind him to make sure that nobody was following him. It was with a heavy heart that, during this promenade, he tossed the book with the cut-out section containing the box into a litter bin. He turned round once more. The street was deserted. He quickly left that place. He often changed direction, in an effort to deceive the people tailing him whom he could not see. Carrying the two remaining books in his right hand, he did not stop until he reached a building with a sign:

HERE DEAD PEOPLE TALK

He went in. No one checked his identity. In a big library readers were walking around freely among the overstuffed bookshelves. They took down books at will because every book had a magnetic security strip which protected it from being taken out of the building.

Making sure that he was not being followed, Rinaldo went up to his favorite reading place. He left the two books he had brought with him on a shelf amid others.

"No one will ever find them again!" he thought, pleased with himself.

To make the books he had brought along as inconspicuous as possible, he marked them in pencil with false catalogue numbers TA4112 and TA4113, similar to those on the surrounding volumes. As he was making ready to leave, he stopped in surprise. He caught sight of Danilo seated at a separate table. His head bent, the bony youth was reading and did not notice anything around him.

Rinaldo walked by taking care not to do anything to attract Danilo's attention. Out in the street he remembered his strange encounters with Danilo. They only knew each other's names from the roll call at lectures. Rinaldo walked on in a bad mood. He was in no hurry to get home. Without He felt very lonely without Natasha and Ari and eagerly awaited their return. Instead of going home, he went to the railway station to write down the time of arrival of their train.

He had reached the railway station before he realized that he had left his pencil in the library. He ran back there. The pencil was still there where he had left it, beside the concealed books. Once more, he set off for the exit. Danilo was no longer there. The books he had been reading lay closed on the table. Rinaldo again looked behind him. When he was quite sure that nobody was watching, he picked up one of the books. He was amazed to read the title:

MEDICINE IN ANCIENT EGYPT

He ran a casual glance over the text:

remedy to stop crying - the use of dead flies - cat's ointment - ointment for burns - crocodile ointment.

"What a load of rubbish!" he smiled, about to put the book down. At that moment he spotted a chapter heading: **POISONS**. His eyes widened. He started to read from the middle of the book:

The beautiful empress gathered together a collection of all kinds of poisons and opiates. To ascertain which of them was least painful, she tested them on prisoners condemned to death. She concluded that fast-acting poisons always caused a terrible sharp pain, while less painful poisons acted too slowly. She then changed to experiments with poisonous animals...

Rinaldo sat down at the table. He turned back several pages and continued to read:

Eight hundred and eleven different doctor's prescriptions are known and seven hundred medicines. These are:...

He ran down the list quickly.

acacia, ...calamus, ...alabaster, ...garlic, ...onion, ...musk or colchicum autumnale, the blood of various animals, ...vinegar, ...

He stopped short here.

musk or colchicum autumnale, the blood of various animals...

"Good God. Colchicum autumnale and the blood of various animals set down one next to the other, on a list of seven hundred medicines, listed completely haphazardly. — Colchicum autumnale or musk. Colchicum autumnale, colchicum," the young man muttered distractedly, his eyes moving from page to page.

every physician knew how to treat one illness and no other. Many neighboring peoples were surprised at this unusual division. In Egypt there were eye doctors, dentists, doctors for ears and doctors for internal diseases.

...methods of growing hair on a bald head ...

...gout was a very widespread complaint, especially among the wealthier classes. The medicines they used often had a toxic effect, and so were banned.

...surgery...

Lifting his head, Rinaldo only then noticed that one of the closed books bore the title:

COLCHICUM OR DOG'S DEATH

This was the poison the old man had told him about in prison. A slow-acting poison that does not kill until a week later. Rinaldo felt his heart pounding with excitement. He read for some time, quite entranced. He was conscious of nothing else around him.

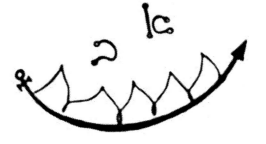

42
The Puddle Which Made Dogs Growl

VICENA HAD TROUBLE concealing his excitement. At the end of so much effort, the secret was at last beginning to unravel.

For days now leading police experts had been combing the garden of the State Administration Centre to no avail. Every inch of turf had been searched and marker arrows stuck in it. Every pebble had been overturned. The entire area under investigation had been signed with a maze of string tied to small impaled stakes. Nothing had been found. Tracker dogs were going round in circles, following the same route José had once taken for his walks. Disturbed peacocks dispersed to the farthest corners of the garden. Vicena was discouraged, yet still determined, and he decided to supervise the search personally. Whenever he had visited the Centre earlier, he had spent his time in meeting rooms. On this occasion, he was surprised to find himself in the garden for the first time. The dark blue feathers of the peacocks melted into an emerald tone with a copper sheen. All around there were trees the like of which could be seen nowhere else in Rome. Some of the trunks forked out of the ground like shrubs, while others only spread their branches at a great height. In some places the trees were bent as if crippled or they had hanging red tassels instead of leaves. Lost in admiration at the flora he saw around him, Vicena caught sight of a gnarled tree with no leaves. Hanging from its branches in long threads were blue buds. It was the time of year in Rome when nothing flowered. The grass lawn between this strange tree and the pathway was covered with a large puddle. The tracker dogs were still busy sniffing round the garden to no effect. They started growling as soon as they approached the edge of the puddle and then continued snuffling their way along the gravel path. No one paid any particular attention to the puddle, which caused the dogs to growl.

There was general consternation when Vicena suddenly stepped into the water. Ignoring the fact that he was wearing low-cut shoes he led one of the dogs across the puddle towards the unusual tree. He was quite sure that José had walked this way on dry ground before the rains descended and created the puddle. When it had crossed the puddle, the dog suddenly started barking. It stood on its back legs and placed its front paws against the tree. It started clawing at the bark of the tree like a mad thing. The police investigators ran over.

In a hollow of the tree where its branches forked, they found a folded piece of paper. They did not dare open it or the damp paper would tear. All they could make out on the back were letters written in ink which had run due to the moisture. Vicena gestured to indicate that the investigation was now at an end. It was then that he realized that his shoes were full of cold water. As he walked away, he turned once again. High up in the bare branches, amid the blue blossoms, birds' nests stood abandoned. He looked in the direction of José's office. Behind the closed window, he could make out dead flowers.

By the following day a report on the letter they had found written in Galatian and certified translations by several sworn court interpreters lay on Vicena's desk. The writing had been completely ruined by the rain and winds. However, the experienced investigators managed to reconstitute the manuscript. Vicena trusted nobody. He went through the translations carefully, placing them one next to another. He compared every single word. Beginning with the salutation

Dear brother Demetrakos

right down to the signature

Emperor of the Galatians

and found that there was no difference at all in the translations. But in the middle of the letter, where the paper was folded, the damage was too great for the sentence

Three young men... set off... to...the emperor...

to be restored in its entirety.

"So that's the poison you were talking to me about?" Vicena frowned. "Will those three young men help each other or are they rivals?"

The handwriting expert confirmed that José had not written the letter. But José's fingerprints were found on the paper. It was unusual for ordinary fingerprints to stay for such a long period. Fortunately, José used to write with a fountain pen and often traces of ink remained on the tips of his fingers.

"My friend, you came from some place in the country!" Vicena was certain. "To be precise, some village in Galatia!"

It is a fact that city children do not pay much heed to trees. Trees lining busy city streets are usually ringed with iron railings to protect them. It is only village children who play in trees and keep their secrets there.

Vicena knew that José had got the letter from somebody and was at a loss how to get rid of it. The sole place where José had felt free was in the garden of the State Administration Centre. But as he did not wish to destroy the letter himself, he had allowed the elements to do it for him.

"Rinaldo is one of the three!" Vicena clenched his teeth. "All I have to do is find the other two. Before that, we'll check just how much this Rinaldo knows!"

Even now he could not free himself of self-reproach in that he had signed that special authorization for José. He worried that the proof they had come upon might link, first José, and then even him, to the conspiracy.

He had to smile as he saw that the case itself was leading towards a general cover-up. The fingerprints they had discovered pointed to no one specifically. The man who had once gone by the name of José Alkorta had completely different prints. The mysterious Galatian who had used the name and documents of José Alkorta as Minister of Education had never had to deposit his fingerprints with the police.

43
Time Of Cold Rains

THE BAD PERIOD of gathering black clouds and tedium had lasted for weeks now. Cold rains, driven by winds, descended upon fell upon Rome. The sky was gloomy and lowering, with no birds or light for weeks. The cold spread through the empty streets and covered the buildings with a damp grayness. People withdrew into their homes, keeping out of the grip of the bad weather. The streets and promenades were deserted.

After their holiday in the north, Mrs Shapiro and Ari returned to Rome. Rinaldo was supposed to meet them at the railway station. Rain fell during their entire journey. Settled back in her comfortable seat, Natasha had not a care in the world. She knew Rinaldo was in love with her and that he would certainly be there to meet them, however bad the weather.

The train was half an hour late getting to Rome. As she alighted from the compartment, Natasha did not see Rinaldo. She spent some time looking around for him. She concluded disappointedly that Rinaldo had not come.

Cold rain splashed down on them at the station exit. Natasha was wearing a warm coat with a fur collar. But her shoes let in water. She was so cold she no longer had any feeling in her feet. Ari started to cry. Sharp gusts of wind whipped up sheets of water in the street. Rinaldo was not in front of the station either.

A taxi cab was standing not far away. Natasha and Ari ran over to it. As they got into the old car, Natasha was shivering with the cold. She told the driver the address and asked him to turn up the heating.

"When'll we get home?" Ari asked through his tears.

"When you stop crying!" Natasha retorted.

She took a make-up mirror out of her purse and turned it towards Ari. "Take a look at yourself! That's what a big cry-baby looks like."

Ari turned his head aside angrily. His tears turned to grumbling. Natasha peered through the misted windows in disappointment. "Rinaldo, why didn't Rinaldo come?" she asked herself. "I must have offended him when I turned him down."

She was filled with dejection and regret at having hurt the young man's feelings. She was sorry that she had been rude to him. Exhausted from the long journey, Ari was cranky and irritable, which put Mrs Shapiro into an even worse mood. Luckily, they were nearly home. She decided to bath Ari first thing and sent him off to bed.

Darkness was falling. Although early afternoon, Rome was already sinking into the murk. The trees swayed beneath the driving gusts of wind.

"Just let's get home!" she thought, tired out.

All of a sudden the vehicle came to a halt. A blinding red flashlight forced them to shield their eyes. An armed policeman with a white helmet emerged in front of them. The irritating light was extinguished for a moment. The pain in the eyes subsided. Blocking their path, the policeman stood there, silent and threatening. Behind him stood another policeman, stiff-faced and signaling to the cab driver to move off. The whole street was under siege from these men with their terrifying, stiff appearance. A blue torch flashed suddenly. The driver, upset, had already looked back in his seat to see how best to turn the car round.

"Mama!" Ari screamed. "Mama, that's our house!"

Without warning, the boy leapt out of the car. For a second, everyone was rooted to the spot. Running fast, Ari had already dodged between the armed men. He was rushing towards the front door.

A whistle rang out. The nearest policeman raised his pistol. Stilling his hand, he pulled back the trigger with his forefinger.

"No!... Ari!... No!..." Natasha chased after her son.

They barred her way. Ari was still running on.

"Ari, no!...Don't shoot at the child!..."

There was a terrible crack. With outstretched arms, Ari fell face down on the pavement. The boy's body did not move. Only his legs twitched for a few seconds as if in a ghostly attempt by the corpse to get up. Blood spurted from a neck wound. The rain continued to beat down.

Mrs Shapiro was struck dumb. The pain she felt forced her to her knees. Half-fainting and helpless, she gazed at her son.

The pouring rain looked horrifying in the brightness of the circular flashlight. Every illuminated raindrop was clearly outlined. Endless jets of water shone in the opaque night sky. Blue and red lights turned on and off at regular intervals. No one moved. Stiff under their white helmets, the policemen cut off all access to the house and the dead boy.

At this point Rinaldo appeared at the door, with a blanket thrown over his head. He had been beaten up and they were dragging him along with his hands tied behind his back. The irritating spotlight of strong red light moved over the street. The thick blanket hid the distorted face beneath. The swellings resulting from heavy blows and the blood running out of his ear remained hidden. His head rolled from side to side, unconscious. The lurid blue light lit up the entire scene for a fleeting moment. Staggering, Rinaldo gave few signs of life. They dragged him to the rear door of a vehicle with darkened windows. Then they returned and threw a tarpaulin over little Ari. They rolled up the tarpaulin with the boy's body and threw it into a second car. Despite the unremitting downpour, they hosed down part of the pavement, which, had it been dry weather, would have retained the bloodstains. After removing these traces, they vanished. The street once again sank into a comforting cloak of darkness.

The dark-skinned taxi driver got out of the car. It was pouring down. But he not only took his time, he also seemed to be moving more slowly on purpose. With slow steps, he went up to the woman who was still on her knees. He raised the unconscious Natasha to her feet. Her arms hung down lifelessly. Her head had dropped down onto the stranger's shoulder. The man felt the warmth of her forehead on his neck. He took her in his arms. Her long face was covered with wet locks of blonde hair. Her unbuttoned coat revealed a crumpled dress. Her muddy knees were slightly apart, and the silk stockings on her beautiful legs were torn. The taxi driver carried her into the cab. As he looked at the house, he saw that the doors were still wide open. Cool as a cucumber, he walked slowly through the heaviest rain to the door. Taking the key out of the inside lock, he closed the door and locked it from the outside. Then he returned to the car and put the key in Natasha's purse.

The battered vehicle set off for the hospital. Tied to the inside mirror, the weasel's tail jerked to and fro. The rain continued relentlessly.

44
A Man With No Friends

THE DAY AFTER Rinaldo disappeared, Danilo returned home earlier from lectures visibly upset. He found old man Vogeler sitting by the hearth. He was drinking tea made from basil, inhaling the aroma of this medicinal plant. He believed that basil could repel sad thoughts. As if sensing death, the old man spent a lot of time by the fire. Danilo interrupted this peaceful atmosphere as he hurriedly approached.

"Mr Vogeler, I told you about that new odd friend of mine."

"You mean the one who never mixes with anyone?" rejoined the old man, lifting his eyebrows. "His name's Rinaldo, isn't it?"

"Actually, he isn't a friend. But something's happened to him. He should have been at lectures today. If he doesn't get the professor's signature, he'll lose the year. I went to his home. Everything's locked up, no one answers. I asked the neighbors. They're not saying anything, they just shrugged their shoulders. They looked aside as if something terrible had happened."

The old man still said nothing.

"Mr Vogeler, you look as if you know something. I beg you; tell me what's happened to Rinaldo!"

"These are evil times. Our emperor Bonifacio is sick. And that's made everyone connected with the government very touchy at the moment. They do not fear for the emperor's health, but for their own privileges. Don't you think it's more sensible to wait till matters improve?"

"But, Mr Vogeler, it'll be too late then! Help me! Put me in contact with Vicena, please!"

"With Vicena, no less!"

"Yes, with him!"

"Vicena's too important a person. Who are we two to talk to him? A student and a frail old man! That's what we are!"

"You're the only person who can help me now! A man's life depends on it!" Danilo was trembling.

Saying nothing for quite a time, the old man finally spoke: "All right. But I tell you, we may never see each other again!"

The old man turned his wheelchair to go out of the room, leaving the frightened youth behind him.

The smell of basil and the smell of fire filled the room.

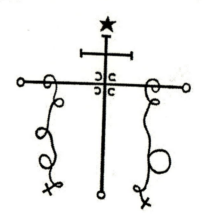

45
Poison

A FEW DAYS LATER, the police sergeant with the scar on his left cheek turned up at the Vogeler property. He was silent. With greeting him, he signed to the young man with his eyes that he should get in the car. He did not say a word during the drive either. The silence was broken only by the ridiculous announcements over the radio receiver.

In front of the State Security building, jets of water were gushing from the gaping mouths of the bronze dragons. The dark raindrops splashing down on the monsters heralded misfortune. The sentries with drawn swords stood motionless. The policeman stepped sharply up to a high-ranking officer, who was wearing white gloves. Around the left upper arm he wore a blue band. He gave a cold, menacing look. Silently, with quick, deft movements he frisked Danilo. Nobody said a word. Then they climbed to the first floor escorted by the frowning officer. He went ahead of them assuring them free passage through the checkpoints along the extensive corridors. Two troopers with tasseled shiny helmets stood in front of a huge oak door on the first floor. As the officer stepped forward, they separated and open the door.

The balding man sat at a large desk in the middle of a spacious room. He did not move. After they were inside, the heavy door banged shut behind them. The Minister of the Interior gave Danilo a searching, icy look. The two men who had brought the young man in stood to one side. Danilo stood there alone before Vicena, who remained silent. As he met this threatening gaze, Danilo went numb. On the wall behind Vicena's back hung a portrait of the emperor in a wooden gilded frame. Next to it the national coat of arms. On the other side of the room there was a standing globe and a large map of the world. Little flags bearing the cross and eagle were planted opposite other pennants with the lion and the sun in the area of the south-eastern wastelands. Danilo recalled the stony desert and the locusts. A blue area bordered with barbed wire penetrated into enemy territory. **Response to the Enemy.**

"Have you any idea at all, young man, where you are?" Vicena cut into his reverie.

Danilo gave a start. Once more he saw the cold, beady eyes before him.

"My name, sir, is Danilo. I was born in…"
"I know all that!" Vicena's voice resounded.
"I'm here about my friend Rinaldo…"
"I know that, too!"
"Sir, no one could tell me what has happened to my friend."

Vicena did not speak. Instead he stared expressionlessly at the apologetic young man.

"Please sir, I managed to get in contact with you through the good offices of the man I work for."

"I know that!"

"If I have already been successful in that, may I know what has happened to Rinaldo?"

The all-powerful minister did not bat an eyelid. He looked Danilo straight in the eye mistrustfully. The fingers of his left hand drummed on the desk top. After some time had elapsed, he said through clenched teeth:

"Attempted murder! Poisons!"

Danilo's face took on a resolute set.

"Sir, I know a thing or two about poisons. If there's just one thing I would ask of you, it is to see that poison."

No one spoke. Danilo looked at the minister with his penetrating blue eyes. Vicena nodded. The officer went up to a cupboard by the wall. He took out the lead box found in Rinaldo's room. Very cautiously he removed the lid. He poured some of the powder into a smaller receptacle and handed it to the young man. Danilo sniffed the poison. Then he spread it around with his fingers and sniffed again.

"This is musk, sir! Nothing else! Musk or dog's death, as it is popularly called. Musk mixed with cinnamon, ginger, pepper and…"

"I know that!" Vicena broke in acidly. "You didn't expect it to be mixed with sugar, did you?"

"But, sir, it's not a poison, it's a medicine! A perfect medicine that could save the holy emperor's life!" Danilo was almost shouting.

The face of the Minister of the Interior darkened. The officer took a step towards Danilo. In a flash Danilo had shoved a handful of the powder into his own mouth. Vicena instinctively reached for his revolver. His mouth dropped open in amazement Danilo had swallowed the poison. The officer was rooted to the spot. The sergeant had turned white as a sheet. The scar on his face was quivering. All three men, flabbergasted, stared at the thin young man. In order to persuade them of the truth of his words, Danilo swallowed a second handful of the life-saving poison. Vicena rubbed his nose. There was a deathly hush in the room.

"Sir, I have to see Rinaldo. If only for a moment!" Danilo pleaded.

Vicena rose to his feet. Upset, without uttering a word, he walked several paces beside the desk.

"So you're one of the three young men!" he thought to himself. "That was now patently clear. I've been waiting for you! Now all I have to do is find the third!"

He sat down again. For a moment his lips twisted. Still saying nothing, he scratched his forehead above the eyebrow. He nodded to the officer and the sergeant to lead Danilo away. The questioning was over.

They hurried out of the room. The sergeant was a worried man as he stepped along. He slowly pulled himself together as he saw that there was no change in Danilo. He was not vomiting, nor losing consciousness.

When he was left alone, Vicena took the box with the poison. He gave it a little tap with the tip of his index finger. He still could not believe that it was none other than Rinaldo who had found a remedy for the emperor's condition.

46
We'll Both Survive

DANILO WAS USHERED into a small room. Apart from a wooden bench and a rickety table there was no other furniture. In a short while Rinaldo appeared. Weak and black and blue from his beating, his hands tied, he staggered towards the table. He was dressed in a dirty prison uniform. Danilo stood beside him.

"Rinaldo, why were you following me?"

Rinaldo started weeping quietly, his head resting on the table. He made no reply.

"I saw you, Rinaldo, in the library reading-room. You were hiding there waiting to pounce on my books!"

"Danilo, that was pure coincidence! I swear! I'd left my pencil behind!"

"I met a man in prison…" said Rinaldo confusedly between his sobs. He dared not look at his friend. "You'll never believe me! Everything conspired against me! But I swear to you, I wasn't following you! I just wanted to make a name for myself. But I didn't follow you! Believe me!"

"How did you prepare the medicine?"

"I didn't! I found the box in a cellar. For days I tried to find out what it was made up of, but without success. It was only when I saw your books in the library that I realized the truth."

"Is the ratio correct?" Danilo asked.

Rinaldo lifted his head. His eyes were cloudy and bloodshot. He was unshaven and his face swollen and dirt-pitted. Above his bloodied right eye there was an infected open wound.

"I asked you, is the ratio correct!" Danilo repeated.

Rinaldo gulped down his own saliva.

"Yes!" his eyes gleamed for a brief moment. "Yes it's correct. I'm sure of it!"

"Then we'll both survive. And you'll become famous!"

Danilo turned on his heel and hurried out.

47
A Starry Sky

FOR A LONG TIME that evening, Vicena tossed and turned in his bed, unable to get to sleep. The pile of screwed up papers found in the wastepaper basket in Rinaldo's room was driving him crazy. The entire inquiry had been initiated because of those scribblings which no sworn court translator had been able to decipher. Many of the sheets had been scorched down the middle as if they had been held too close to a candle flame.

"Those papers, it seems, are a load of rubbish!" thought Vicena.

Yet the very next moment his suspicions were aroused: was that not too easy an excuse? It was hard for him to admit to himself that he was still at a complete loss where those papers were concerned. He was so upset that he could not sleep. He did not have a clue what to do with Danilo and Rinaldo.

He felt that it would be better to sit and wait for the third young man to show up. On the other hand, he feared that Bonifacio's health could take a turn for the worse. If that poison was really the remedy, then Rinaldo could cure the emperor. In spite of Danilo's naiveté and ineptitude in coming to visit Vicena he had saved Rinaldo's life.

Among the multitude of official documents, Vicena had managed to get his hands on the report compiled on students who had applied for the University. Beside the names of Rinaldo and Danilo there were poorly erased question marks and the stamp *Read!*. It was not clear to Vicena how the experienced sergeant could have overlooked two young men who he had discovered just as they arrived in Rome. He decided not to reveal to the sergeant that he knew about his omission. He held him in a trap of silence and kept that secret for a better occasion. It was only by chance that he had not missed the whole case.

Vicena finally managed to get to sleep around midnight. But there was no peace for him even then.

He found himself in the unreal land of Galatia, which had been overrun by peacocks. Nothing could be seen for the huge numbers of birds spreading their tails. These fanlike tails even covered the starry sky whose the shining stars were only visible through the feathers. The leading star was a large-eyed spot shaped like a death's head.

He awoke, screaming with terror. However unusual this might appear, Vicena was superstitious. José had known this and had once presented him with a book of dreams. Now, in the middle of the night, half-awake, Vicena remembered that gift. He got up, put on the light and went towards the bookcase. He re-read the dedication on the flyleaf:

To my dear friend
With best wishes for his birthday.

He nervously turned over the pages until he finally came upon the interpretation of his dream:

The peacock is a symbol of beauty and the power
of transformation. It is believed that the beauty of the
colors of its feathers comes from a transformation of the
poisons the peacock sucks up when it kills snakes.

"Damnation!" Vicena grumbled in an undertone. "This is going to drive me mad. Poisons? Is that possible? Peacocks and poisons?"

He was taken aback when he read the final sentence:

To dream of a peacock means to have an untrustworthy friend.

Vicena was by this time wide-awake.

"Problems should be dealt with fast, one by one! And immediately, before it's too late. As soon as possible before those three cost me my life."

He sat down at his desk. He wrote quickly, with jerky movements of the hand.

In the thick of the night, he put together an order to the *Confidential Institute No.2* to deport Danilo to Galatia.

"There are no peacocks in that wilderness for sure! But plenty of snakes to compensate!"

Vicena did not relax until he had signed the document. Nothing could stop him now except superstition. He burned the crumpled papers from Rinaldo's waste-paper basket in the empty fireplace. Then he took the letter José had concealed in the tree. Once again he read the unfinished sentence:

Three young men... set out... to... the emperor...

He rolled the letter into a ball and threw it onto the weak fire. He did not want to hear any more about José, about Danilo, or about Rinaldo. He switched off the light and went to bed. Released now from a worrisome burden, he quickly fell asleep.

48
King Of Fire And King Of Shadows

OLD MAN VOGELER sat by the fire, alone in the dark room. Warmth flooded the area around the hearth that night.

Flames licked around the glowing logs. Sparks were flying. The objects round about gleamed as if they, too, were alight, in the heat of the blazing fire.

Danilo was no longer in Rome.

The old man added dry sticks to the fire. He poked the heated coals Red-hot tongues flared up. The wood and the air were burning. The red flames fought with the wild orange fire. The clear red fire, bright and pure like celestial love, was disappearing into the dirty orange fire which looked as if it was burning underground and destroying all in its path. In the overheated vortex, fire was consuming fire.

Vogeler had tried several times, without success, to find out from his cousin, a police sergeant, what had happened to Danilo. All written information concerning Danilo had been destroyed. There was not a single indication remaining that Danilo had ever been in Rome. Even the police sergeant could not unravel the mystery surrounding his sudden disappearance. All clues had been removed in such a perfect fashion that the sergeant judged it prudent not to make any more inquiries about Danilo.

Vogeler grieved for the young man. He could not rid himself of the suspicion that Rinaldo was responsible for Danilo's disappearance. Vogeler was sure that he would never see Danilo again and that Rinaldo would become a person of some importance.

It was peaceful. The heat made Vogeler more and more drowsy. In the silence all you could hear was the even crackling and occasional flaring of the fire. The far, unheated corners of the room were cold and dark.

Old man Vogeler's head dropped down onto the armrest. His gentle, immobile face shone in the warm, red glow. He fell asleep and died in that sleep, with a smile upon his face. The shapes in the fire and the objects illuminated by it danced on the walls, only to vanish in the kingdom of shadows.

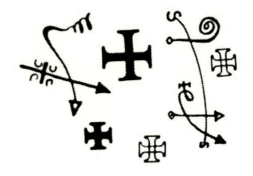

49
The Book Of Wisdom

possessed by the Romans, but not by the Greeks

Achieving perfection within a short time, he had a long life;
And because his soul was dear to the Lord,
He quickly rescued him from the evil around him.
The multitude sees this, but do not understand;
It does not occur to them that kindness and mercy belong
To those chosen by the Lord.

(Book of Wisdom, 4.13-15)

AS IT WAS WRITTEN in some ancient books, Rinaldo was saved from wretched captivity for the second time. In preparing the miraculous medicine, he succeeded in delivering the holy emperor from his pain.

Naturally, it was whispered that Rinaldo secretly worshipped some other gods, and not the god who protected the empire. Consequently, many at court were convinced that the young man would once again end up in prison. But the medicine was effective. Emperor Bonifacio recovered quickly. His face grew bright and the world seemed a better place to him. Out of immeasurable love for his people and his physician, he stopped persecuting those other gods. He conferred upon Rinaldo the elevated titles of Minister of Health and Minister of Education. True, the emperor did not actually do this in person, but the court sycophants, sensing that a new age was coming. The emperor's good spirits and favor were obvious. Smooth-tongued men began to suck up to Rinaldo and heap honors upon him. And so it was that by the grace of God and the will of the holy emperor Rinaldo reached a position of authority. It had never happened before that one man was appointed to two powerful positions. The double appointment to be both Minister of Health and

Minister of Education was the subject of an official decree, certified with the signatures of all the imperial advisers. Copies of the decree were sent to all corners of the empire, however remote. The name of the young minister was uttered and his story told with due reverence and admiration throughout the world.

This reputation thus reached the small village in Catalonia where Rinaldo had long since been forgotten in people's conversations. But upon hearing this news, the villagers were disturbed. First it was said that Rinaldo had been born under a lucky star. That he was in cahoots with unclean spirits, that he was attended by fairies, that he spoke animal language, and that snakes obeyed him.

Back in Rome, his enemies admired him for having succeeded in life.

50
The Boy Who Wanted To Be Cuddled

WHEN DANILO AWOKE, he realized that he was lying on a floor mat. His hands were tied behind his back. In another part of the room, two men were having an argument in a language he did not understand. Dumbfounded, he suspected that he was not in Rome. A woman in a shabby dress was cooking and serving the men. The entire room was full of the smell of tobacco and grilled peppers.

The younger of the two men was disheveled and unshaven. He was shouting and banging his fist on the table. The other, clearly the man of the house, neater and much older, nodded his head in agreement. The guest wolfed his food down. Burping loudly, he raised his glass in a toast.

"Heavens, where am I now?" Danilo sat up.

The younger man rose from the table, stretching his arms out joyfully. Beaming, he came up to Danilo and kissed him on both cheeks. He stank of dried sweat and brandy. He patted Danilo on the shoulder and turned him round, bound as he was, to face the head of the household as if to persuade him that the young man was, indeed, alive. Perplexed, the old couple looked at him in silence.

He took a crumpled receipt out of his pocket. He did not untie Danilo until the old man had signed it in a shaky hand. Happy at having completed this task successfully, the quickly said goodbye and left. The head of the house did not see him out. He shut the door complaining that he could hardly wait for this unpleasant man to go. Still puzzled, he turned and looked pityingly at the young man.

"Do you understand me?" Danilo asked.

In place of a reply, the woman started setting the table. The old man simply shrugged his shoulders. Then he gestured to the young man to sit down and eat. Danilo had a headache. He was really hungry. He sat down. Outside it was beginning to get dark. So they had been waiting for him to regain consciousness.

They served him thick soup and pickled peppers. The old man sat facing Danilo, smiling at him good-naturedly. Danilo put his head down and ate, avoiding the gaze of the unknown man.

"What's old man Vogeler doing now?" he wondered, concerned. "Does he know where I am?"

He was overcome by lack of sleep and drowsiness. Toward the end of the meal, this unpleasant feeling left him. He looked at the kindly old man. Behind the old man's back, a cross and a picture of a Roman officer were hanging on the wall. The spoon fell out of Danilo's hand. He got up astounded.

"Major! My major!" he pointed at the picture and then at himself. "It was he who saved me!"

The old woman burst into tears. The old man covered his face with his hands and mumbled something.

Danilo was struck dumb. He went over to the wall. Beside the large picture of Major Karamark in uniform, there was another one of two boys in the shallows of a river hugging a foal. The boy who was stroking the foal with his hand had the same features, the same eyebrows and the same look as the major in uniform. The affectionate foal was standing in the middle, tottering on its weak legs. The other boy, who looked as if he wanted to be cuddled, pushed his cheek right up to the foal's neck. Putting both his arms round the animal, it seemed as if he was whispering something tender in its ear.

Danilo's eyes widened in amazement as he looked at the picture. When he turned round, he saw the old woman weeping. She was holding an officer's saber in her hands.

"José Alkorta?" asked Danilo, pointing to the boy fondling the animal.

The woman started to sob. She beat her hands on her breast. "Vesko! Vesko!" Her crying turned to a wail.

The old man extracted a folded letter from behind the picture frame and held it out to Danilo. The man dropped to his knees in front of the wall. He sobbed, his face in his hands.

Danilo could not deceive himself any more. The smile of the late minister under the dark green sheet was the same as that on the face of the boy fondling the young horse.

Outside, night had already fallen.

51
Rushing River

EARLY IN THE MORNING a priest came to Danilo.

"You'll be fine with us!" he said in a harsh accent. "We waited for you to come round. We wanted to taker you over to care for you immediately, but this wasn't possible. Our religious order is different from order in Rome, which is why they don't like us. Whenever something happens in the village, the authorities only trust that old man Karamark because his son was an officer. A major even, so they say."

A horse and cart clattered over the road which was full of holes. The driver shouted angrily at the horses.

"Did they have any other children?" Danilo asked the priest.

"No, he was an only child. Though, they did foster an orphan as well."

"Was that the boy in the picture?"

"Yes. His real name is Belisario. But we called him Vesko. We were very fond of him, but it didn't help. All of a sudden Vesko ran away. He never got in touch again. We don't even know whether he's alive. But from that day those people have never had any peace. I think they are tortured by pangs of conscience, even though they were kind to the boy. Nothing can comfort them. They even think that the death of their only child was God's way of punishing them for Vesko running away."

"Is Major Karamark dead?"

"Yes. He was killed in Rome, shot in the back. The rumor goes that he was unarmed at the time. None of our people ever had much luck in Rome. Where are you from?"

"From Thrace."

"As a foreigner, you did not make your fortune in Rome either. They simply take advantage of us and throw us aside when we're of no further use to them. The Romans are cruel. They didn't banish you to your own country, but here to us, in Galatia. They hold the power and they just play around with human lives."

Danilo handed the priest the letter, which the major's father had taken out from behind the picture frame.

"Please translate this for me!"

The coach driver cursed and shook the reins furiously. The priest followed the text with his forefinger. The rushing river could be heard in the distance.

"Translate the passage about José Alkorta!" Danilo explained.

The coach driver was swearing even louder now. Danilo was overcome by the freshness of the morning.

"I was in trouble," the hard accent of the priest was heard. "In much greater trouble than you can ever imagine."

The horses snorted outside. They were having difficulty moving through the quagmire. The priest read carefully:

"A stranger helped me. All I know is that his name was José Alkorta. Whenever you pray and light a candle, please mention his name, too. I went to Rome twice to thank him, but to no avail. He refused to receive me, so I don't even know what he looks like."

A chill came over Danilo. He recalled the day that the major summoned him. And then the drive.

"The morning hours have golden mouths." The words rang in his ear. He remembered José's smile in the morgue.

On the weed-covered slopes a flock of scraggy sheep was visible from the road. The cold weather lent the area a depressing gloom. Thick swirls of mist covered the infertile fields. Boys in ragged trousers and woolen sweaters were leading animals to the watering hole. They moved slowly. Tired from lack of sleep, they took the flock into the mist. The sound of the rushing river gradually drowned out the shouts of the boys.

52
Walled-up Windows

THE SOUND OF hammer blows and the shouts of workmen resounded down the corridors of the State Administration Centre. They were walling up the windows and door of an empty office that gave out onto the garden. Because of the resulting din, the disgruntled employees could hardly wait for the working day to end. A secretary was frittering away her time out of boredom in the reception area on the first floor. She knew that she would not have anything to do that day, that the minister would not be receiving any visitors, so she was painting her nails. Federico sat at the other end of the room.

"José's gone, and now his room has, too."

"I'm afraid that's life, Federico!"

"And now, to top things off, a water pipe's gone and burst. They're jinxed. It's like there's a curse on everything. They're going to have a job fixing that pipe. For a while he said nothing. He was angry at them for removing the last traces of José."

"Whose stupid idea was that to move the archives down there? It was a good office. It's a shame they're turning it into a storeroom. With no windows, it'll look like a tomb!"

"There are people paid to think about things like that," the secretary assured him in a bell-like, carefree voice. She was far too preoccupied with her pretty nails to pursue this pointless conversation.

Federico heaved a sigh and stared listlessly at the ceiling.

"Stupid cow!" he thought, furious with himself for having even started the conversation with her. "I wonder if anything exciting has ever happened to her in her life. She isn't even capable of understanding what's going on around her!"

In the adjoining room, Rinaldo, the newly appointed Minister of Health and Education, was going through the papers of all the deceased.

He was so engrossed in his work that he was not even aware of the noise the builders were making. Careful not to miss anything, he ran his forefinger slowly down the list of unknown names. For the umpteenth time he came back to the bare heading:

SHAPIRO, ARI ... Died accidentally while running across the road.

He hoped that the information on Ari was false. But the date of death was precisely the same as the date when Natasha and Ari were supposed to have returned from their holiday. The day when he failed to meet them. The day when they arrested him. Was it possible that all this had happened on the same day?

Since that day he had tried in vain to discover what had become of Natasha. Her name was nowhere to be found. He had combed lists of taxpayers, bank account holders and debtors, water supply users, and members of citizens' associations. He had gone through the telephone directory. All to no avail. Natasha Shapiro was neither among the living nor the dead.

In an effort to recall Natasha's face, he saw that of Kristina. Or rather a hotchpotch of Kristina's eyes and Natasha's face. Everything looked mixed up. He could no longer distinguish between illusion and reality. He doubted that he would ever find Natasha. In his disappointment, he got up from his desk and went over to the window. He drew back the curtains. It looked as if something was not going well with the work outside. The noise had stopped. The workmen were having a break. They were sitting in a circle, drinking beer. Oblivious of the break, one of them was still breaking up a concrete foundation beam with his hammer.

"How can I appeal to Vicena for help?" Rinaldo was wondering.

He was sill filled with fear at the very thought of the man. Rinaldo increasingly linked his detention in New Future more with Vicena than with Abaddon. Abaddon was just the prison warden and, naturally, subordinate to Vicena. Vicena was more powerful than any of them.

Vicena and New Future represented a nightmare from which Rinaldo could not free himself. Even now, the windows of the State Administration Centre grounds were reminiscent of those in the New Future prison yard. The builders passing each other bottles of beer reminded him of the prisoners rinsing the pebbles. The builder who stayed on working was crawling like that disfigured prisoner. It was as if the long since experienced scene was happening all over again. The workmen were getting to their feet. At that very moment, Rinaldo turned pale. He remembered his anguished suspicions that that they were taking him to the madhouse instead of prison. Terrified, he ran into the next room.

The secretary and Federico stood up in fright. They stared at the minister wide-eyed.

"You, Federico, you come with me at once! You, Miss, phone the head of the asylum to wait for me! To wait for me, in person, with Natasha Shapiro!"

The secretary could only gape at him in astonishment.

"Who is Natasha Shapiro?" she managed to get out.

"He'll know very well who I'm talking about!"

They left in a hurry. Federico turned on the siren and drove as fast as he could.

After a long drive they stopped in front of a shabby building in the suburbs. A pile of coal that had been delivered made access difficult. Coming to meet them was a middle-aged man with a forced smile on his face, short with a thin moustache. He was wearing a crumpled doctor's white coat, which was dirty round the hem. Rinaldo strode past him angrily. Perplexed, the stranger was forced to turn on his heel and run after him. Despite his fear, he tried to show a warm welcome.

"We're so sorry, Minister, but the warden and his deputy had to go somewhere urgently for half an hour. They weren't here when the call came through that you were on your way. I'm the duty doctor."

"You were told to wait for me here with Natasha Shapiro!"

"She's all ready, Minister. She's in the building. We're sorry about the coal. I told them to bring it in immediately. But everyone gives their own orders. It'll all be settled by this evening. You can be sure of that! Don't let that upset you!"

Rinaldo was walking fast, a frown on his face. The doctor now turned to give the driver a smile:

"We'll soon reach the ward! It's no distance!"

Federico gave him a resentful look. Not speaking now, the doctor led them into the building. The nurses and porters stood lined up along the corridors they went down. Following the doctor, Rinaldo and Federico were approaching a white door at the end of the building.

Rinaldo motioned to Federico to wait for him in front of the door. As he entered the small room, Rinaldo half-closed his eyes for a moment. The dull light bulb on the ceiling threw a weak dark yellow light. Although it was illuminated, the windowless room remained in a yellow twilight. Natasha was waiting inside. The nurse beside her was combing her long, blonde hair with calm, slow movements.

Natasha was sitting there, head up and motionless, lost in her own thoughts. Her dreamy, kind eyes were lifeless. Her face was still beautiful, but her hair was beginning to get dirty. Her pale forehead bore lines, which it had not had before. Her head remained absolutely still. All you could hear was her light breathing. Every now and then her, dead eyes would blink. Her lips were curled in a slight, frozen smile, in a way she had never smiled before. With light movements, the nurse drew the comb through her hair.

As if suddenly waking up, Natasha slowly turned her head.

"I know who you are!"

The nurse was dumbfounded and could not move. It was the first time she had heard Natasha speak.

"You ruined my life! You killed my son!"

Following this moment of effort, blunt fatigue once again spread over Natasha's gaunt face. Her lips trembled, but she did not have the strength to speak again. Down her deformed, spasm-gripped cheek, a tear rolled. The nurse resumed the hair-combing procedure as if nothing had happened.

All the objects in the windowless room were yellow from the dim light bulb. There was a picture of a seacoast hanging on an empty wall. With yellow branches of yellow trees on the yellow coastline. The waves of the sea were yellow, as was the sky above. The yellow glow from the room's artificial light blunted all emotion and transported people into eternal sleep.

Clasping his head in his hands, Rinaldo moved towards the exit with leaden steps.

"The medical findings!" he turned to the doctor.

"Here they are, Minister. We got them all ready for you."

Leafing through the pile of papers as he walked, Rinaldo turned numb when he read the word *querulatria*. He knew that this was not the name of an illness but yet another false title, invented to deceive anyone inquiring about the patient concerned.

"Well, that's life for you!" Federico gave a sigh.

The duty doctor, visibly upset, escorted them to the main door. He knew that it was a serious offence if you were caught absent from your post during working hours.

The minister said nothing. He felt a headache coming on. The bars on the windows of the asylum reminded him of the bars in New Future. Memories of the prison suddenly turned into the mad scream of the old man:

"I am the Chosen One!"

The duty doctor wiped the sweat from his brow with a handkerchief.

"Minister, I assure you that this all happened out of the blue!"

53
Division Of Power

**All hands are stretched out towards God,
But He only takes the hand of him whom He loves
(British Museum, Papyrus 10508, Ankhsheshonqy, 392)**

AFTER TOURING THE ASYLUM, Rinaldo could not marshal his thoughts. His headache was getting worse. Voices that had come to him in the past now echoed in his ears.

"I am the Chosen One!" repeated the voice of the toothless old man from Colchida. "Minister, I am the Chosen One and I assure you that this all happened out of the blue!"

Rinaldo clamped his hands over his ears. Horror-struck he realized that the voices were coming out of his own head.

When he got back to his office, Rinaldo found an opened letter on the desk. It was from Kristina.

"My God!" he thought. "Nothing has happened to me for months. And now everything's happening in one day. Both Natasha and Kristina, and the same day."

"I assure you that all this has happened out of the blue!" he softly repeated the malicious words.

Along with the letter there was a pierced and torn envelope. Rinaldo was furious that his letter had been opened. But he calmed down when he saw that there had been no bad intention involved. The letter had been opened when it arrived in the same way as all official letters directed to the State Administration Centre.

Rinaldo,

Life brought us together and separated us in a cruel way. My new life started in Rome. It is possible that you think I behaved badly towards you when we met again. It would have been a mortal sin, you know full well, if I had behaved any differently.

Now my husband is in trouble. I have no one else to turn to except you. Johannes had a slight fever. The ambulance came just in case. But through somebody's mistake, he ended up in an isolation facility. My daughter and I are powerless to do anything.

Rinaldo, only you can help us! Only you can get Johannes out of that graveyard!

Kristina Dirken

The words jumped and jumbled up in his mind. Rinaldo settled in his chair and threw his head back. He closed his eyes. Teeth clenched, he breathed heavily. It was as if he had lost everything. He was quite alone now, without Kristina, without Danilo, without Natasha. A spiteful voice kept ringing in his head, mocking him. "Tonight, Kristina, your friend went completely mad!"

Suddenly he heard a gentle woman's voice.

"Don't be frightened! Don't forget that you have the power. Everyone admires you! You cured Bonifacio and in return he gave you power over people. You have become Emperor of the Galatians!"

"I'm not mad!" Rinaldo screamed in terror.

"Of course, you're not," said the female voice soothingly. "You are Emperor of the Galatians! People admire you because they know you are smarter than them."

"But that's not true! Johannes laughed at me!"

"You shouldn't let that bother you any more. You prayed that your enemies would perish and that prayer was answered. No one will ever laugh at you again! For you are Emperor of the Galatians!"

His headache showed no sign of letting up. He tried to focus his thoughts on Natasha, but the malicious male voice came back to him.

"Your friend is sad tonight. Yes, tonight your friend has completely become Emperor of the Galatians."

All of a sudden his nostrils narrowed. He straightened up and reached for a sheet of paper. In an illegible hand he quickly wrote down the following words:

Due to the general dangerous situation, the isolation facility is hereby placed under complete blockade. This emergency measure remains in force until a new order is issued.

    State Administration Centre
    Ministry of Health

He summoned Federico. After he had been handed the order, Federico waved a silent goodbye and left quickly. Rinaldo moved away from the desk. He paced up and down the office, the palms of his hands pressed against his temples.

"Natasha... Natasha... Why did they ruin her lovely skin that way?"

She did not even turn her head. Once again he heard the voice of the toothless old man. But thus time, instead of mocking him, the voice spoke admiringly.

"You do indeed have all the power. Tonight you have become Emperor of the Galatians!"

Rinaldo dropped his hands. Grabbing his coat, he went outside.

That evening, as he was returning home, Rinaldo turned the car in the direction of the isolation facility. As he neared the hospital, he had to change direction. Policemen in white helmets had taken control of the entire area.

Weapons at the ready, they had the hospital surrounded. All access roads were sealed off. Powerful searchlights flashed ominously in the dark night. There were no passers-by. The whole deserted area looked haunted and bewitched.

54
The Distant Unknown

AN OIL PAINTING had been hung in the conference room of the State Administration Centre. On a large wall the face of José Alkorta looked down among the portraits of generals and high-ranking clerics. On the floor beneath the picture two big vases of flowers had been placed. José was standing proudly holding a book in one hand and an illuminated globe in the other. With a noble smile on his face, he looked above the heads of the visitors at unknown distances.

The conference room had not been used for official purposes over a number of years. Regularly maintained, the empty room served once a week as a poorly used museum for the public. The rare visitors paid no heed to the painting on the wall. The impression was that José Alkorta, albeit surrounded by flowers, was increasingly fading from people's memory.

No one paid any attention to the untidy youth who turned up one dark day in a group of visitors. Separating off from the group, he walked around slowly, inspecting the art objects displayed in the corridors. As he entered the conference room, the young man suddenly broke into a run. He was clutching a little bottle tight in his hand. He stared at José like a madman. As he threw back his arm while running, he tripped over one of the vases of flowers and fell. The stranger started screaming on the floor. Acid from the opened bottle spread over his face. The guards ran up when they heard the crazed howls. They did not know how to help the disfigured young man who was dying amid the scattered flowers. A white trail left on the floor by the acid ran over burned petals and stems.

José stood there, with his elegant smile, staring into the unknown distance above the heads of the guards who had gathered there.

That same day, when order had been restored, a young major in civilian clothes inquired after José. They pointed to the painting. An elderly cleaner was trying unsuccessfully to erase the marks of the acid from the marble floor. The stone had cracked and was covered in holes over which the destructive fluid had flowed and mixed with blood. In a new, tight-fitting black suit, the major walked with measured steps, as if sensing evil, and went up to the picture. He recognized Vesko. He knelt down beside the picture and burst into tears.

"Calm down, sir!" the cleaner comforted him.

The major did not hear.

"Dark forces assailed that man!" the woman continued. "The madwoman who murdered him in the nursery school managed to get away. But the Good Lord punished this one today."

"Vesko!" the major sobbed. "My Vesko! My little Vesko!"

He started to shake. He tried to get up, but lost his balance. He thought he was going to faint. The cleaner ran over to help him.

"Help!" she cried.

Losing consciousness, the major grabbed the woman by the shoulders for support.

"Help!"

The guards ran in, this time with pistols in their hands. Thinking that the man was out of his mind and was attacking the woman, they shot the major from a distance.

"Dark forces! Dark forces!" the woman screamed as if she had lost her senses.

She stretched her arms out towards the painting on the wall.

"See what you've done! This is your work! We all loved you, and you brought only misfortune!"

"I didn't mean to!"

The woman was struck dumb. She stared at José in amazement. Horrified, she closed her eyes and crossed herself. Again she heard the same despairing voice.

"I didn't mean to!"

"I know!" — one of the guards was consoling his less experienced colleague. "You had to act the way you did! Rome is full of crazy people."

55
Tale Of The Emperor's Recovery

WHEN HIS IMPERIAL MAJESTY has recovered, it was announced that he would receive all his ministers, governors, generals, mayors of big cities and representatives of his beloved people.

On the appointed day, the visitors started arriving from all corners of the immeasurable empire. The whole scene was one of dignity and honor.

The large hall at court filled up with a host of dignitaries. They were smiling in their formal clothes and there was a flash everywhere from their jewelry made of gold, pearls and precious gems. War decorations glittered on official uniforms. Bare women's shoulders gently shivered in low-cut dresses. There was the sound of laughter on all sides. But it was a false gaiety. Behind the forced smiles, fear lurked. Something untoward was happening. Apprehension about probable changes, distinctly unfavorable for their way of life, had crept into everyone. They were scared because they sensed that something evil was about to take place.

Keeping his hands in his pockets, Vicena stood to one side as he usually did. Examining all these important people with his beady eyes, he smiled maliciously and dignified no one with a greeting. Such vulgar behavior was extremely unusual, but this was his way of showing his power. After José's murder, he did not seem to give a hang about anyone any more. He observed the guests around him listlessly, barely concealing his scorn.

"You see, our Rinaldo reached these heights without any help at all," an overweight, overdressed woman was chirping to her escort. "But where is he from? Nowhere. Some people say from Catalonia. And he's got no father and no mother to be happy for him today. To see what their son's achieved!"

"Well, madam, that's the way it goes! That's how life seems to arrange itself. This hall here tonight is some sort of orphanage. If you were to separate those who had a happy childhood, there'd be almost nobody left. Orphans are marked, madam!"

"And he's so good-looking and so kind!" she continued bubbling with excitement.

"He never seems to age at all!"

"Yes, madam, I've heard that from a lot of people."

"Oh, don't be like that! Those are only remarks made by jealous people. Rinaldo made his way through life all by himself!"

"That's nothing, madam. Just take a look at those generals at the other end of the hall!"

There was a group of hairy Galatians standing by the wall. Judging by their wild appearance, it looked as if they had just thrown wolf skins over themselves. Everything about them was untamed, their hooked noses, their bony faces, and their penetrating, unfriendly gaze. Tall and broad-shouldered they stood there proudly, in their silk general's uniforms.

"But they are nothing but savages! Galatians and who knows what else!" muttered the woman in alarm. "My dear man, they should not be invited to such gatherings, among decent people!"

"Yes, madam. But these people are the confirmation of our power. It's only in powerful states that a foreigner or a slave can scale the imperial heights. And Rome will only last as long as that is the case."

The dark eyes of the Galatians flashed under their bushy eyebrows. The Romans feared men with eyebrows that joined in the middle, for they believed they were possessed of two souls. The bony bodies of the tall generals were graced by new silk uniforms decorated with the cross and eagle, symbols of the Holy Roman Empire, embroidered in gold.

There was a festive air about that day. The sapphire stone floors had been polished, and the hall was hung with flowers from the southern seas. The blue marble walls were draped with huge flags and imperial coats-of-arms. But few people paid any attention to all this. If they had, they would have discovered an unusual triangle with an all-seeing eye drawn inside it. And a cross whose upper bar had been replaced with a chain link.

The generals noticed that they were being stared at by a sagging man and an overweight woman. They nodded an acknowledgement in their direction with a forced smile. The man and the woman graciously returned the greeting. In Rome it was very important to keep smiling. Nobody liked miserable people.

The sounds of lively conversation from the distinguished guests could be heard on all sides.

"Madam!" a tiny, bony, wrinkled woman addressed her.

This woman had so far kept herself separate from the crowd, her face uplifted. With a proud movement the first woman turned her head to look at the small woman.

"Oh, it's you, my dear! What a pleasant surprise to meet you here!"

"I'm so very happy to see you again!"

"My dear, what do you think of the Dirken tragedy?"

"But I know nothing about that!" her eyes opened wide in curiosity.

"You haven't heard about it! Is it possible? It's terrible! You must know her husband, Johannes, God rest his soul!"

"Don't tell me something's happened to him? He hasn't died, has he? Been killed?"

"Not yet! But he won't last long! He's got this terrible illness. They didn't know what to do with him, so they put him in the isolation facility. And you know that's a graveyard for the living!"

"Johannes Dirken among the lepers? How could that have happened?"

"A mistake in procedure, my dear," the woman sighed. "His wife Kristina begged everyone she knew to have her husband moved. But you yourself know what people are like. Especially in circumstances like that."

"Poor Kristina!"

"Oh, my dear, that's not the end of it! The very same week, her babies got a skin infection. Poor little girls! They didn't even live till their first birthday."

"Was it bad?"

"Yes. It all began when their skin suddenly started to dry up and age. Within ten days they looked as if they were fifty. They were buried in secret. They say it was awful to look at them so disfigured!"

"But I didn't know anything about it! We only arrived in Rome today. What a terrible misfortune! And what became of Kristina?"

"She hanged herself! That's why no one talked about it."

"Oh, my dear, you see what life does to you. But why should the children suffer? You simply never know when your time has come!"

The sharp roll of imperial drums interrupted the buzz of conversation. Fanfares rang out. There was dead silence. Emperor Bonifacio entered the hall with his armed bodyguard in plumed helmets. He was immediately followed by Rinaldo, draped in a red cloak. Behind them came troopers and twenty-four wise old men in long white robes. The emperor walked with a brisk step, a smile on his face. After the moment's surprise at seeing him so hale and healthy passed. There was a reaction of general delight. The hall resounded with loud cheers and applause. The solemn procession had almost reached the throne. This square area, raised by ten emerald steps, was guarded by twelve golden lions, who emitted a sudden fierce and false roar if anyone other than the emperor tried to approach.

The emperor mounted the throne in the atmosphere of general pomp and cheering. As Rinaldo came near, there was a muffled growling sound. He did not stop. The golden lions fell silent. Moving onwards, undeterred, the minister stood next to the emperor.

The twenty-four wise men encircled the foot of the throne. Dividing off into two groups, the plumed bodyguards stood on each side. Everyone held their breath.

"Look at Rinaldo, sitting on the right hand of our holy emperor!"

Their joy knew no bounds.

"Our Rinaldo's such a good man!"

"My God!" Vicena muttered to himself. "He's gone quite mad!"

Vicena knew by heart every word of the report on Rinaldo he had got from the Recruiting Office. He knew that Rinaldo suffered from schizophrenia, but he was not sure how the illness would manifest itself. He cast a concerned look at Rinaldo whose face was distorted by spasms. With their lunatic expression, his eyes were firmly fixed on some point in the distance.

"What a noble face!" the guests chorused admiringly.

"And what dignified bearing!"

Rinaldo shifted his glance to Vicena. The Minister of the Interior bowed his head. The young man's heart gave a jump. He, Rinaldo, the indigent prisoner, had become the most powerful man in the entire earthly kingdom. He had power over everything — distant provinces and the city of Rome, blue seas and snow-clad forests, all the windmills, all the animals and all the peasants. Rome's top officials bowed down before him.

The crack of drums again broke up the clamor. Silence fell, and then everyone burst out singing.

"We trust in Thee, O Lord," the words ran round the hall.

In line with the rules on paying tribute, the emperor neither got up nor sang himself. He sat proudly on the throne, the sides and armrests of which were formed by two emerald eagles. In one hand the emperor firmly clasped the scepter, and in the chubby fingertips of his other hand gently caressed the eagle's stone plumage. Their beaks open wide, the eagles clenched jade balls in their talons from which pale green smoke was billowing forth. The smoke hovered just above the base of the throne, from which sweet-smelling oils exuded from concealed openings. Rinaldo stood beside the throne. He said nothing, but just looked on. His head wound head had long since healed, but the furrow remained. A scar testifying to ill fortune and bad memories. He squinted from his menacing, taut face with its frozen muscles. He looked as though he was about to tear his enemy to pieces. Finally, he caught sight of Johannes.

"We trust in Thee, O Lord," the hymn echoed. "The whole world respects Thee, Eternal Father."

The subjects sang on, in thunderous unison, the song of their love and hope.

Rinaldo's eyes flashed deep in their sockets. His lower jaw was stiff with fury. Teeth clenched and terribly angry, he stared at the man who was laughing at him. He could have killed him with that look.

Terrified and disheveled, Johannes pressed himself up against the wall, as far away as possible from the lepers. But they caught sight of him. Vicena gave a nod. The ghostly figures fell upon Johannes, muttering crazily. His staring eyes clouded over. Instead of their customary self-confidence, there was death in them now. Two of the figures grasped him firmly by the arms. He tried to get away and screamed. The living dead men began piling up bricks and binding them with cement to the live man. Hammer blows rang out. The cement gradually started to set. The weight crushed down upon his legs. The lepers went on building and reached the level of his chest. Then they released his arms. Johannes uttered cries like a wild beast as he tried to push the wall away. The hard bricks tore the skin off the palms of his hands. The veins on his neck stood out as he howled, his bloodied hands waving in the air. He gave a despairing shriek. His jaws gaped open. A drooling apparition with a rotting nose walked over to him and spat down his throat. The shriek was drowned. Filthy hands closed his mouth. His eyes rolled. His arms fell limp. The wall pressed in on him. Blisters appeared on his upper lip, above the teeth. Immured and spattered with his own faeces, Johannes did not die. The disfigured lepers, bewildered by the sight, moved away from this horror.

The anthem was over. The emperor raised his hand and touched his crown, topped with a gleaming golden eagle and cross. A spotlight ran over the crown and created the impression of burning fire. As he moved his hand, the emperor's bracelet also caught the light. In the same way as bright stars sparkle differently from dimmer ones, so, from a distance, the blinding light of the eagle and cross shone differently from the dull gleam of the bracelet. Although encrusted with precious stones, the bracelet was made of copper. On the copper base an engraved winged snake encircled the emperor's wrist, swallowing up its own tail in the fire of a red ruby.

The twenty-four wise men fell to their knees before the figure seated on the throne. They bowed down, saying:

"Oh master, you are worthy once again to receive tribute, honor and power!"

Bonifacio was radiant and proud as he viewed his subjects. At a given sign, a heavy hammer struck the bell in the main belfry. The same sound was heard again as a muffled echoing reply came out of the distance.

"What a wonderful man our Rinaldo is!" — these words could be heard on all sides.

"What a noble face!"

Rinaldo's eyes sparked. His left cheek stretched upward. The left side of his lips distorted into a hideous grin.

"I am the Chosen One!" he whispered contentedly. "I am truly Emperor of the Galatians!"

Ringing bells were heard from distant towers. Their echo stifled the end of the day. Beneath the red glow of the setting sun, the outline of the towers sank into the darkness. The good news of the emperor's restoration to good health was being broadcast far and wide. The bells rang to the glory of the all-powerful ruler. The stone rulers and stone generals were no longer visible in the murk. The evening bell rang out from a thousand belfries. Only the blackbirds flew across the sky, harbingers of the night.

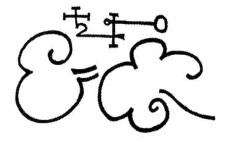

56
Hiding From The Voices

A WEEK AFTER the festivities to celebrate the emperor's recovery, something happened that no one expected. It was well past midnight and the night watchman was standing at the entrance to the State Administration Centre, very upset. High above his head, on the façade of the building, the illuminated stone cross and eagle were to be seen. The watchman repeatedly looked around him in apprehension. He held a torch in his hand which he kept turning on and off inadvertently. He only pulled himself together when he heard the sound of a vehicle in the distance driving this way at high speed.

A large black official car suddenly drew to a halt. Vicena jumped out of the car, slamming the door behind him. He hurried towards the night watchman.

"Where's Rinaldo now?" Vicena asked angrily.

"In the garden, minister! He seems to have gone stark raving mad!"

Vicena went into the building. The duty telephone operator stood perplexed at the reception desk.

"Have you called for an ambulance?"

"No, minister. The matter is too delicate. That's why we informed you first."

"You did the right thing!" Vicena nodded, moving towards the reception desk. "Call a doctor immediately!"

"You mean, the madhouse?" muttered the telephonist.

There was no answer. In the wake of the night watchman, Vicena was already well down the familiar corridor. The night watchman opened the French windows and led Vicena into the garden.

"What are you doing at this time of night in the garden?" Vicena asked.

"Hiding from the voices!"

The gravel paths were lit by low-placed lamps. This was the first time Vicena had come into the State Administration Centre garden since the investigation into the death of José Alkorta. His eyes strayed unconsciously to the leafless tree where José had hidden the message about the three young men. The night watchman appeared to be leading him in precisely that direction. As they came near the unusual tree, the watchman flashed his torch into the branches. Vicena stood rooted to the spot. There among the branches stood Rinaldo. Blue flowers with long fringes were hanging beside his head. His face was twisted with effort. He shielded his eyes from the torchlight with his right hand and held on tightly to the tree with his left.

"What are you doing up there?" Vicena shouted.

"It's the end of the world!" Rinaldo whimpered. "I can't stand it!"

The night watchman was still pointing the torch at Rinaldo who was unsuccessfully fending off light with his right hand. Vicena considered coming closer, but the large puddle was still there in front of the tree. He had no intention of getting his feet wet for Rinaldo.

"How do you know it's the end of the world?"

"People have gone mad! Don't you see what's going on? Don't you see that people have lost their minds?"

"So what! Who cares if they've lost their minds?"

"A red-headed woman is spreading misfortune! She wants to destroy the human race! I hid myself away from the sound of her voice!"

"And where did you hide?"

"Here! That woman doesn't dare come into this garden!"

"You see!" Vicena yelled. "She can't be that powerful if she doesn't dare come into the garden!"

"But she's the queen of the locusts!"

"You're not telling me that you're afraid of locusts?"

"The locusts will survive! Locusts are holy creatures! When mankind has disappeared, the locusts will still be here!"

"Then it won't be the end of the world." Vicena tried to calm his fears.

"The world will survive! Only human beings will vanish!"

"Yes! But I can't stand it!"

The sound of a siren came from the street. The blue and red lights of an ambulance lit up the dark sky.

Vicena had never liked Rinaldo. Ever since the young man had been given so much authority, he had gone strange in the head. Vicena put this down to Rinaldo's illness and forgave him everything. Even now he felt pity as he watched him standing powerless in the tree. He wanted to help him.

"Come down at once! When the doctors take you away, there'll be no hope for you. So come down this minute!"

"Who are you to order me around!" Rinaldo countered. "I am Emperor of the Galatians! I hold a much higher position than you!"

"Then stay in that position!" Vicena waved him away.

As the watchman continued to light up the branches of the tree with his torch, Vicena walked back towards the exit.

A doctor and a couple of male nurses ran into the garden. The stronger of the two orderlies climbed up the tree. He wrenched Rinaldo roughly from the branch, which he had been clutching for dear life. He gripped him firmly round the neck and pushed him down into the arms of the other nurse waiting down on the ground. Rinaldo did not struggle. He watched calmly as they carried him over the puddle and laid him on a stretcher.

The doctor gazed at Rinaldo in consternation. He summoned up the courage to approach him only when the orderlies had tied his hands. After this moment of confusion, a triumphant smile spread across the physician's face.

"Now we're going to take good care of you, minister," he murmured, well pleased. "You already know our institution. We've moved the coal out of the yard. Now everything will be just as you like it!"

He cleaned Rinaldo's right forearm with alcohol, then picked up a ready prepared syringe. With a deft movement of the hand, he injected him with a tranquillizer.

57
Battle In Heaven

THE WASTES OF distant Galatia were in the grip of a silent snowstorm. A thick fog covered the deserted plateau and wrapped itself around an isolated stone monastery. Danilo the convert was keeping watch in the dark chapel. Only the flickering candle lit his pale, sickly face. He was so exhausted he could barely stand. He was shivering with the cold. There was a smell of wax and incense in the air.

"Our Father, grant Thy peace to those who suffer!" the echo of his voice could be heard.

All the walls around him were painted with angels. The position occupied by each angel reflected his power in the heavenly hierarchy. Thus, painted thrones floated above cherubs, seraphim above powers, dominions above authorities, and principalities above archangels and angels.

"Our Father, grant Thy peace to those who suffer!" his heartfelt plea was repeated and bounced upwards off the dark walls.

The voice died away and silence reigned. Even the wind seemed to have stopped blowing. Danilo's body was racked with fever. With his last ounce of strength, he cried out once again.

"I call upon Thee, O Father! Hear my voice, Lord!"

He became quiet once more. It was freezing cold. The skin on his fingertips had cracked. Blood spurted from the open wounds. He paid no heed. He bent down and moved the candles for the living to the place reserved for the candles for the dead. The cold flames quivered.

"Our Father! Receive the souls of the wretched! Still the troubled minds of your servants! Receive unto Thyself those who are buried alive, infected, poisoned, frozen, crazed, slaughtered, strangled, burnt alive, stabbed, walled up in stone. And bless those who have perished in a terrible fashion, for Thy mercy is endless. Hear the cry of those who suffer, for evildoers have conquered the world!"

He looked up at the dome where night prevented him from seeing the thrones and cherubim with books in their hands. All around, under the cloak of darkness, he was followed by the painted eyes of seraphim with flaming hearts, powers holding earthly globes, dominions scepters, authorities holding spears, principalities with crowns, archangels with swords and angels with souls.

It was only then that Danilo noticed that the trail of blood from his fingers had stayed on the candles for the living, which he had switched to the place for the candles for the dead. A ghostly flame was trembling and shadows flew violently across Danilo's face. The faint light gradually weakened and faded into the darkness. Danilo's face could no longer be discerned.

Suddenly, there was a thunderclap. Flashes of lightning cut through the night. A green flaming ball illuminated the black sky for a single moment. From this bright light, silvery green snow fell upon the earth as far as the eye could see. The eerie, bare branches of a lone tree stood out in the snowbound wilderness. As though there were no fog, and no night.

"Our Father!"

Then, for a second, everything sank into darkness. The green light gleamed out of the torn leaden clouds one more time. There was more thunder. In the middle of winter the entire firmament shook. The roaring sounded like the charge of mounted horsemen. Their hooves churned up the earth. The clashing of swords was heard. The snowstorm whipped into a fury. Bugles rang out. The screaming wind drowned them out. Then more deafening rolls of thunder. The whole earth was aquiver.

Danilo's lament echoed through the storm, and overcame the thunder:

"And forgive them their crimes, for they know not what they do! But put an end to this atonement! Put an end to this terrible suffering and return hope to us!"

Lightning flashed for the last time, but no thunder was heard. The candle flame grew smaller as everything would be snuffed out. But after a momentary paroxysm, the flame burst forth brighter and stronger. Of all the painted figures, only the one nearest the flame — Archangel Michael slaying the monster with his sword — was visible. Everything fell quiet. Green blood ran down the blade of the sword which, itself, seemed to be on fire.

Danilo wept with exhaustion. With tears in his misty eyes he beheld the archangel and the slaughtered beast. The weakened body of the young man collapsed onto the dark stone floor. It remained curled up like an embryo in the dark, lifeless.

The wind died down. The chapel was filled with the gentle peace of crackling candles. The snow fell lightly.

The quivering light of the flame illuminated the kind face of the archangel. Scattered golden rays gleamed around his head. The archangel was as beautiful as God himself.

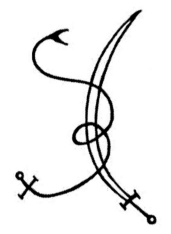

58
Song Of Songs

The winter is past,
The rains are over and gone.
The flowers appear on the earth;
The time of singing has come.
The voice of the turtledove is heard in our land.

ABOUT THE AUTHOR

Mihajlo Kažić, a Serb, was born in Pristina in 1960, and completed a civil engineering degree in Novi Sad.

In 1985 he was awarded a Fulbright scholarship to study in the US, and obtained his M.Sc. and PhD in engineering from the University of California in Los Angeles in 1986 and 1988 respectively. He worked as a science researcher and lecturer in Novi Sad, Los Angeles, Corvallis, OR., and in Paris and Stuttgart (Germany). Kazic has since worked with several construction companies in Germany; since 2003 his home has been in California.

Emperor of the Galatians is the author's first work to be published in English. The book was originally printed in Germany by Kiepenheuer (Leipzig) in 1993.

Kažić has written two other books, both of which were published in Serbian and in German. *Broken Journey*, was published by Prosveta (Belgrade) in 1996, and by Suhrkamp (Frankfurt) in 1996; and *The Gates of Heaven*, was published by Prosveta (Belgrade) in 1998, and by Suhrkamp (Frankfurt) in 1999.

Author web site: www.kazic.org

Printed in the United States
29286LVS00002B/1-66